2 SIDES 2 THE RAINBOW

By: UNIQUE WATERFALL

Published by: Unique Waterfall through CreateSpace.com

Edited by: PR Literary Services

Cover design: Daysha Holloway

Email the author: mz.waterfall10@gmail.com

Below ISBN refers to print edition:

ISBN-13: 9780988294301

WITH GOD ALL THINGS ARE POSSIBLE!!!!

First and foremost, I want to thank my Heavenly Father sitting on high.

Thank you, LORD, for this opportunity and ability that you have bestowed upon me with writing this book. I am nothing without you and I am everything with you! Your Grace, Mercy and Love is everlasting. I love you, LORD! Amen.

To the three loves of my life! My 3Ds: Day, Dar, and Dai. I love you always. This is all for you guys.

To all of my friends and family, thank you for supporting me, for believing in me, and walking this journey with me. It has been a great adventure. I am forever grateful to each one of you. I love you and there is so much more to come.

This book is dedicated to my Snickadoodle, Q. I love you and I always will. Thank you for all that you have done. For raising the bar and loving me the way that you do.

Forever your Waterfall.

CHAPTER ONE

"Oh, shit! Damn, girl. Oh, you like that? Let me go a little faster," Angie said as she rode Khai's strap.

They had been fucking all night since running into each other at Delacor.

"Hey, what's up with you, girl? You know I've been trying to get with you? Why you playing games?" Khai asked Angie.

"I'm not playing games with you," Angie said giving Khai that don't go there with me look. I didn't think you were serious with me."

"Well, let me show you how serious I am. Come go home with me," Khai said as she walked up closer to Angie.

"Home with you, really?

Hell yeah!" "Trust me, you won't regret it," Khai stuck her hand out for Angie to take it.

"Ok," said Angie as she grabbed Khai's hand and followed her out the door and to her place.

Straight to Khai's bedroom, they wasted no time.

"Man, you not playing are you," asked Angie.

"Hell no, I told you I wanted to get up with you," replied Khai.

Khai pulled Angie into her arms and began to kiss her. In and out their tongues danced around. All the while, they were removing their clothes to begin the love match that they both were anticipating.

Khai laid Angie down on the bed and began to caress Angie's body. She kissed her all over from head to toe. All of Khai's movements were slow and passionate. This turned Angie on to the fullest. Slowly, Khai rose up from Angie's beautiful body and went to desk in the corner of her room.

"What are you doing?" asked Angie looking puzzled.

Khai turned to her, gave her a little wink and said, "Don't you worry about that. You just lay there lookin' sexy."

With that, Angie lay back on the bed and waited patiently while Khai did whatever she was doing at her desk.

Khai returned to the bed facing Angie and laid her body on top of hers. She started kissing her again, softly on the lips. Then slowly Khai inserted her strap into Angie's throbbing pussy.

"Oh, yes, girl," Angie moaned as Khai went in and out with slow thrusts.

Back and forth, she went into Angie's pussy, making it wetter with every stroke.

"Hey baby let me get on top," Angie whispered.

"You want to ride this dick, baby?"

"Mm, mm, yes!" Angie moaned.

Angie got on top of Khai's strap and slowly slid her wet pussy all the way down to the base. She started to bounce on it. Up and down, she began riding her dick like a pro.

"Yeah, baby!" Khai shouted. "Give it to me! Get this dick, girl!"

Khai was in pure heaven as she watched Angie's beautiful breasts bounce up and down.

"Slow down, girl, you are going to make me cum like that."

"Yeah, that's what I want," Angie replied. "That's what I'm here for. I'm going to make you cum all over yourself," Angie said as she leaned in to kiss Khai's lips.

Faster and faster, Angie rode Khai's strap as if her life was at stake. "Oh, oh, say my name," Angie purred into Khai's ear.

"Angie! Angie! Yes, Angie!" Khai growled. "Mm, mm."

Khai took Angie's breasts into her mouth, sucking on her nipples. First, she sucked one at a time, then both at once.

"Oh, girl, tell me how you like this," Angie asked.

Unable to speak, Khai just licked and flicked the top of Angie's nipples. She twirled her tongue around them as Angie bounced on her dick. Khai was being taken to new heights.

"Yes! Yes! Oh! Oh!" moaned Angie.

"Oh, yes, oh!" Khai yelled.

They both exploded into orgasm, fulfilling their needs of lust for their bodies.

"Girl, I didn't know you had it like that," said Khai.

"It's more where that came from just wait and see. Whew," Angie exclaimed as she climbed off of Khai.

"Damn, girl, look at all your cum on my dick."

"It's all for you, daddy," Angie purred seductively as she looked around for her shoes and clothes.

Angie started getting up from the bed when Khai grabbed her by the waist.

"Hey, what are you doing? Stay the night with me." she said.

"I can't," responded Angie as she was getting dressed. "I have something to do, but I promise after I'm done, I will be straight over here for round two."

"You better," said Khai, as she walked Angie to the door.

They shared a quick kiss good bye.

"I will be back," said Angie, as she walked into the early morning hours.

"I will be waiting," Khai smiled, as she shut the door thinking about round two. Oh, I can't wait for that one, she thought.

While walking to her car, Angie thought to herself, oh, yes. I will be back for some of that later on today. Angie got into her car and turned on the radio. Usher was playing. She turned it all the way up, blasting it as she drove home. Because, indeed, she was a little freak.

Checking over the contract one last time, Ming made sure everything was in its proper order. She wanted to ensure that there would be no surprises during her meeting. She had always admired DC's work and the opportunity to have her as a client was perfect.

She checked her watch. She was running behind to meet her girls for brunch. They always get together to shoot the shit and catch up with one another's lives. That's something all best friends should do, because it's laughter for the soul.

Ming put the documents in an envelope and made sure her desk was nice and neat before she headed out of door.

While driving to the restaurant, Ming turned on her music. Ciara's *Other Chicks* booms out of her speakers while she zoomed through the streets trying not to be any later than what she was. She made a mental note to herself. Once DC becomes my client, I am going to treat myself to something nice like a new briefcase embroidered with my initials. That would be nice, she thought. It really is time for a new one.

Nayla, Angie, and Rachael were at the table waiting for Ming to arrive. They were chatting amongst themselves about the events going on in their lives.

"Hey, y'all what's going on," said Ming as she arrived at the table. She gave everyone a hug and a kiss as she walked around the table.

"Nothing much. I'm good. What about you?" they chimed in, in unison.

"Sorry I'm late. I was working on some last minute details for this deal I'm hoping to land. It's a new potential client. I really would like to work for her, because I am a big fan," said Ming as she sat down.

"Who is it, girl?" Nayla asked. "Some big superstar? Tell us. Tell us."

"I don't want to disclose that just yet. You know how I am. I don't want to jinx it. Just wait, you guys will see soon."

"Well, we hope you get it girl. Make that money, cha-ching." They all snapped their fingers while dancing to the sound of money being made.

"Speaking of money," Rachael says. "Let me tell you what my RL got for me this week. Some Escada evening sandals with a matching clutch. She only spent $2,000, but that's cool for now. I can't wait to rock them next week at work."

"RL? Who the hell is that?" Angie asked. "And only $2,000? Girl, please, that's more than enough for some shoes and a purse."

"Not a who, but a what," Nayla replies as she put her head down to take a sip of her green tea.

"That's her term for a rich lesbian. She calls them RL's for short," Ming answered.

Rolling her eyes at Rachael, Angie just shook her head.

"Yes, RL is my code," Rachael says looking at Angie. "Unlike you, I get something in return."

"What monetary gifts followed by some cheap thrill? Whatever, no matter how you slice it, you just like me. You just a high price ho. So, hell, what kind of code words do you have for us?" Angie asked.

Rachael laughed, "You really don't want to know what kind of names I have for you."

"You really shouldn't have code names for anyone, but I'm not even going to go there with you. I came to enjoy my brunch," Ming says.

17

"I could think of a code to call you, too," Nayla says while high fiving Angie. "But anyway, let me tell you guys what the hell happened the other day. My sister calls me and says she was on her way over. She said she was in the neighborhood and wanted to stop by. So she gets there and we are making small talk. No biggie. She's telling me what's going on with her blah, blah, blah. I go to the kitchen to get some ice and upon my return, she is in my desk drawer looking for a pen and a piece of paper. So she said. Low and behold, she found my lesbian porn stash."

"What?" Ming asked.

"OMG!" Rachael gasped.

Angie shook her head and said, "That's why you need to get your ass out the closet!"

"Well, what did she say," Ming asked.

"She asked me what I was doing with lesbian porn in my drawer. I asked her what she was doing in my drawer in the first place. She then went on to say she was looking for a pen and paper, and don't try to change the subject. So the first thing I could think of was to tell her that I was doing research for an upcoming project at work."

"Research my ass. Yeah, if only she knew you were the project and you are looking for some female to research you, all right," Angie laughed.

They all burst out laughing together, because they all knew it was true. Nayla had been in the closet forever. She only messed around with femme women when, as she puts it, the urge strikes. This way, no one would ever suspect that she likes pussy if she wasn't seen with a stud. You can't tell a femme is in the life unless you ask or she tells you.

"Well, did she believe you?" Rachael asked.

"I don't know," Nayla responded. "I just closed the drawer and we started on something else."

"Nayla, for real, when are you going to face facts? You are a lesbian! Your whole life is gay, baby. Come on over to the other side," Ming started to sing. "Come over to the other side."

Angie began singing with her, "The other side, we are waiting for you come on. We won't bite, not unless you ask us to."

They all started to laugh and sing, "Come on to the other side."

"Your ass is confused. That's what you are, confused," Rachael professed. "Because, I don't see how you have kept it a secret for so long."

"Yeah," Angie said. "Now, see if you were out like us, you could be getting some good stud love instead of messing with chicks that fly under the radar. You trying to make sure nobody knows. But, for real for real, you shouldn't give two fucks what anyone thinks. Tell them to kick rocks with flip-flops."

"However, back to that stud love," Angie coos. "Oh wee, let me tell you what that's all about. You see, last night, I ran into this stud that I had been seeing around and we talked for a minute. Next thing you know, I'm getting my body banged out. Oh like a Congo drum, girl, shit, I can't wait until part two. She done some tricks that even I didn't know."

Laughing out loud, Rachel said under her breath, "Tricks you don't know? Wow!"

"I'll drink to that. At least someone is getting some," Ming said as she took a sip of her iced tea.

"I wish it were that simple for me," Nayla responded. She then thinks to herself, *I just like what I like.*

"Well, oh, I'm done," Angie said. "I couldn't eat another bite."

Everyone agreed.

"I will be hitting the gym tonight, ladies. Which one of you wants to join me?" Ming asked.

"I can't," answered Angie. "Didn't you just hear me say I am waiting for round two with my stud tonight?"

"Ho," Ming responded. "Just make sure you're not late for work tomorrow. Don't be trying to pull no half day shit, either, because you all wore out."

"Okay, boss lady," Angie said. "I won't. I won't. So, let me go now so I can get started early."

"Damn, girl," Nayla said. "It's just one o'clock in the afternoon. How early do you need to start?"

"Don't you worry about that, Miss In The Closet," Angie joked. "Okay, ladies, I will see you all later in the week. Except you, boss lady, I will see you bright and early tomorrow. I promise." Angie then got up and kissed her friends good-bye.

"I'll go with you tonight, Ming," Nayla said. "What time do you want me to meet you at the gym?"

"Around 6 o'clock, I'll call you just before I'm leaving. Now, don't fake out on me."

"I won't. I won't. Trust me, girl, I will be there."

"Okay, cool," Ming said as she took a sip of her drink. "I have to get out of here, too. I'll see you guys later. Don't worry about the bill, I will pay on my way out."

"Oh, if I would have known that, I would have gotten me a little something else," Rachael said as she took a bite of her salad.

"I am not one of your RLs," Ming interjected. "Know that." She blew the two remaining ladies a kiss and walked to the front to pay the bill.

Rachael turned to Nayla and said, "I would never even want her as a RL. She knows too much about me."

They both laughed while getting up from the table to leave.

"See you later, girl," they both said as they hugged and kissed each other good-bye.

CHAPTER TWO

"I told you, I was going to kick your ass. Look at the score," Stony says to Ray. "21 to 7. Told ya, you can't fuck me with on this game."

"You only are winning by a touchdown. This game isn't over yet, so quit talking shit."

"Watch my dust. Whew, another touchdown. What's the score now? 28 to what? Now what? Ain't no coming back, bro. It's how many seconds left? It's a wrap. Game over," Stony dropped the controller, dancing. "Who's the man? Give it to me. Who's the stud?"

"I'm the stud," Ray said. "That's just one game. How many games have I kicked your ass in? So, okay, you got one."

"Hey, y'all will never guess who was in the store today," PG said.

"Who?" asked Stony. "Some big booty freak that you just gotta have?"

"Yeah," Ray said. "Big titty Tina?" She and Stony slapped hands.

"Yeah, man. A few of them stopped in, but you know how I do. I'll check them out later on this week depending on if something better comes through. But, on the real, no, I'm talking about DC. She's in town and she stopped in to get a few things at the store. She's here on some business. I told her we need to kick it before she leaves."

"Yeah, that's cool. What did she say she's been up to?" Ray asked.

"Hell, with all that damned money and pussy she's getting now that she's this top notch model, it don't matter. Right?" Stony said. "Shit, I need to do a couple of auditions and get me some paper. It wouldn't hurt. I'm fine and I can cook. It's the total package."

"I don't know about fine, but I will give it to you. You can cook your ass off," PG said.

"I know that's right," Ray replied. "Just keep your day job."

"Don't hate. If it wasn't for me when we go out, neither of you would get a girl," Stony laughed. "They come see me. Then, I tell them to bring along some friends for my friends and then maybe we can all be friends."

"Please don't even flatter yourself. I don't need you to get a chick. Miss me with that one. What's my name? PG. And what does it stand for? Pussy Getter. Don't forget."

"Where's the food?" Ray asked. "I thought you ordered a pizza."

"Yeah, I did. Let me call to see what's the hold up." As PG was getting ready to call the pizza place, her phone rang. "Hello?"

"Hey, what's up?" said DC.

"Nothing much," PG said. "Your ears must have been burning. I just got done talking about you."

"Oh really?" DC said. "To who?"

"Ray and Stony are over here. We were just waiting for a pizza I ordered that's taking forever."

"Well, won't you guys come up to Dashes and meet me for a drink so we can catch up."

"Hold on, let me see," PG said while putting the phone on her shoulder. PG asked Stony and Ray if they wanted to go to Dash's for a drink.

"Hell yeah," they both said. "Let's go."

"Okay, DC," PG said. "We're on our way." PG hung up the phone and asked her two stud buddies, "Which one of you is going to drive?"

"I'll drive," Stony said. "I have a meeting in the morning so I can't get too toasted."

"Good, because we plan on getting our drink on," Ray and PG chime in as they give each other dap.

Dashes, was a Lesbian bar/restaurant on the south side of Chicago. It was one of the few places that a lesbian could go, get a drink, relax, chill, and be comfortable in a gay environment. The food wasn't bad either.

"What's up? What's up? What's up?" DC said as she saw her old friends in the front of the restaurant.

After giving everyone a hug and some dap, the friends went inside. At the host station stood a short light skin chick with light brown eyes.

"Good evening. Welcome to Dashes. How many in your party?"

"Five, if you join us," PG said. "But, we can always ditch them and just make it two."

The hostess just smiled showing her deep dimples. "This way to your table," she said as she led the four friends to a booth.

After she handed PG her menu, she leaned in and said, "Maybe later, we can make it just the two of us. I get off at nine. See me before you leave."

"I sure will," PG said. "I promise."

"I sure miss home, I tell you," DC said. "It's good to be back. I see some things don't change."

"You know how we do it baby," PG chimed in.

"It's some fine ass women in here tonight," Ray and Stony said as they looked around checking out the ladies that were there.

There were all sorts of ladies in the bar tonight. You had your pick of anything you could possibly want: tall, dark, short, light, medium, long hair, short hair. Whatever was your fancy, you could have it with no problem from this crowd.

"So, man. What's going on with you?" Ray said to DC.

"Nothing much, man, just doing that model thing. Getting a little homesick."

"Homesick? Man, why, with all that new pussy you're around? How could that be?" PG asked.

"Man, that shit gets old. You never know what these chicks are out for. Most of the time, is it my money or the perks from being with a model. You know traveling the world, that high life. They think they can just get it free. But, I'm not interested in a woman who only wants what I can offer her, not who I am."

"I feel you," Stony said giving DC some dap.

"So, what have you guys been up to?" DC asked.

"Nothing much. Working out and still beating these fools in the game," Ray laughed.

"Getting the ladies, of course," PG said. "Didn't you just see me in action just now, baby?"

"I'm good," Stony said. "Same old thing. Perfecting my cooking skills. What about you? What brings you home and how long are you here in town for?"

"On business, shopping around for a new attorney. I got this recommendation for this one in particular. I'm here to meet with her to see what she's all about, but I'm not sure how long I will be in town. Maybe a few months. Glad it's the summer so we can do some hanging out and I can beat y'all on the basketball court."

"Bring it on," everyone said.

Just then the waitress came over to the table. "Hello, my name is Sonia and I'll be your waitress for the evening. What can I get you guys?"

They ordered drinks and appetizers. They continued to talk and reminisce about old times.

"Hello," Nayla said as she picked up the phone.

"Hey, are you ready," Ming asked.

"Yeah, I'm ready. What time is it?"

"Its 5:30, meet me at 6, okay?"

"Okay, I will meet you there. See you in a few."

"Okay, see you there, bye."

"Bye," Nayla said as she hung up the phone to get ready to meet Ming at the gym. *Oh, why did I agree to go today? My show will be on tonight at 7. Oh well, too late, may as well get out now so I won't back out,* Nayla thought. She grabbed her stuff and headed out the door to the gym.

I have to work off this nervous tension. I don't want to seem too anxious, tomorrow, Ming thought to herself when she heard a thump and felt a pull. "What the hell?" she exclaims. She pulled over to inspect what was going on with her car. She realized that she had just hit something in the road and now had a flat tire.

"Fuck," she said.

Ming got on her phone and called roadside assistance. "What do you mean it's going to take about an hour to get here? I don't have an hour to sit here on the side of the road waiting for you! I don't pay you every month for your services to wait! Do more than what you are doing and get someone out here ASAP!" Ming yelled into the phone then hung up.

"Fuck, who can I call?" Ming said as she looked through her contacts.

Ming hit Nayla's number to tell her what happened, but it went straight to her voicemail. Just as Ming was leaving Nayla a message, a handsome stranger appeared.

"Excuse me, Miss?" the stranger said. "Do you need some help?"

As Ming turned around to decline the stranger's offer, she was suddenly overcome by the stranger's presence. Out the corner of her eye, Ming thought the stranger was a guy and she was not in the mood to have to deal with any heterosexual macho nonsense. But upon turning to face this handsome stranger, she realized that it was a woman. A stud? *Wow*, she thought to herself.

"Excuse me, Miss. Do you need some help," the stranger asked again interrupting Ming's thoughts.

"Oh. Yes, sorry. I was leaving a message for a friend to come and help me."

"Well, you don't have to do that," the stranger said. "I can assist you, if you like."

"I don't want to be any trouble," Ming replied.

"Oh, it's no trouble at all. I will have you off and going in no time. Do you have a spare?"

"I do believe, but I'm not even sure. I have roadside assistance. Since today is Sunday, they are much slower in their response time."

"No problem," the stranger said. "Pop your trunk open and we will go from there."

Ming, doing as the handsome stranger asked, opened her trunk. A slight breeze blew carrying the fragrance that the stud was wearing in her direction. *Mm...*, Ming thinks as her nose is filled with the intoxicating aroma of the stud.

"Yes, you have one back here. This will take me just a minute. Just stand back over there on the curb and I will have you back driving in no time."
"Okay," Ming answered.

"Can you hold my shirt? I don't want to get any dirt on this."

"Sure, it's the least I can do for you helping me," Ming took the stranger's shirt in her hand and slowly ran it by her face. She wanted to smell the stranger's cologne once more.

The kind stranger hiked up the car and proceeded to take the tire off. She was now wearing only a tee shirt that was showing off her fit and muscular body. *Damn*, Ming thinks, as she bites her bottom lip. *Whew, I never knew studs were like this.*

The stranger was also checking out Ming in her pink and grey workout gear, matching from head to toe.

"So, were you on your way to the gym or coming from the gym?" the stranger asked casually.

"Going to the gym," Ming answered. "I was trying to get in a little cardio. I do appreciate you assisting me. I would have had to sit here for an hour and wait for someone from roadside assistance to help."

"No problem. I love to help people whenever I can. I'm just glad I was coming this way to be of assistance."

"So am I. Lord knows I did not want to be sitting here waiting on roadside assistance. Paying them every month is a waste if they can't be there when you need them."

"I do agree," replied the stranger. "But, I'm here now. So, you don't have to worry your beautiful head about it any longer. All done, Miss Lady," the stranger said as she finished with the tire. "And, now you can be on your way."

"Thank you so much," Ming replied, as she handed the stranger her shirt back.

Just as Ming was getting ready to ask the stranger her name, the roadside assistance car pulled up and an old, dirty, potbelly man got out and said, "Hi, I'm here to fix a flat tire. Do you still need help?"

"No, not anymore. It has been fixed," Ming told the roadside assistance guy. She then turned to the stranger and said, "Thank you, once again."

"No problem, baby girl, it was my pleasure."

Interrupting the two, the potbelly man said, "Oh, well, I still need you to sign this form as proof that we came out."

Just as Ming was getting ready to ask the stranger for her name, the stranger turned and walked to her car.

"Please sign here, here, and here."

Before she could finish with the paper work, the handsome stranger was gone. *Damn*, thought Ming, *I didn't even get her name.* The sound of her phone ringing snapped her out of her daydream.

"Now, where are you, miss meet me at the gym at 6:00? It is now 6:30. What's the business?" Nayla asked.

"Girl, you wouldn't believe what just happened. Skip the gym. Meet me at my house. I have to tell you what just went down."

"Bitch, I will be there in ten minutes," Nayla said as she hung up the phone.

"Man, it was good seeing you guys tonight and catching up talking about old times."

"Yeah," Ray said. "It sure was. We are going to have to kick it this week sometime."

"For sure," Stony added. "Just let me know when we all are going to hook up."

"Hey, speaking of hooking up, I'm about to hook up with the hostess tonight so let's bounce."

"Right, I have a meeting tomorrow with the attorney so I do need to get some rest," DC said.

"Me, too," Stony said. "I have an event to cater tomorrow, as well. It was good seeing you guys. I will call you all sometime this week."

The old friends left the restaurant and headed to their cars. But before leaving, PG made good on her promise and stopped to see the hostess.

"Hey, baby, what's your name?"

"Mia," the hostess replied. "What's your name?"

"PG. Now, how about I come over to your place later on tonight when you get off so we could get to know each other better?"

"Sure, said Mia. "Well, my number is 312-995-5371. Call me when you get off and we can take it from there."

"Okay, I will," Mia said. "I'm going to go home and freshen up. I will call when I'm done.

"Cool, no problem, baby girl. Hurry up. I'll be waiting for you," PG reached out and kissed Mia on the hand. "Until later tonight."

"I'll see you in a few," Mia replied.

With that, PG headed out the door and to the car where Stony and Ray were waiting.

"What took you so long?" Stony asked.

"Nothing. I was giving her my number so when she gets off, we can hook up."

"You're going to tap that ass?" Ray asked.

"Of course," PG replied. "She fine as hell and if she wants to go all the way, then PG is going to give her what she wants."

Stony dropped PG off first. "Have fun tonight, man, and be safe," both Ray and Stony tell PG as she exits the car.

"I will. I promise I will. Bye, I'll call you guys tomorrow."

Stony blew the horn as PG headed into the house then closed the door. Once inside, PG started to think about her visit to see Mia. She said her name aloud. *Mia, I can't wait to stick my dick in your pussy tonight, girl. I hope you know what you getting into with me.* PG then starts to get her overnight bag ready for her night of fun.

CHAPTER THREE

Ming and Nayla arrived at Ming's house at the same time.

"Girl, what's going on?" Nayla asked.

"Come on in," Ming said as she opened the front door. "I ran over something on the way to the gym and caught a flat tire," she said as she walked to the kitchen.

"Are you ok?" Nayla asked as she gave Ming a hug.

"Yes," Ming responded. "I'm good. I was kinda pissed off, but I'm not anymore. That's what I wanted to talk to you about."

"Oh, okay," Nayla replied. "Who fixed the flat, roadside assistance?"

"No, girl, that's what I'm trying to tell you. I called roadside assistance and they told me it would be about an hour before they could come and fix the flat. So of course I was mad. I told them they needed to get out there sooner than an hour, because I didn't have an hour to wait for them. So, I hung up from them and tried to call you, but it went straight to your voice mail."

"Sorry," Nayla replied.

"No, it's cool. Just listen. So, I'm trying to leave you a voicemail when a car pulls up. At first, I thought it was some macho guy and I just wasn't in the mood for that. Turns out, it was a stud!"

"A stud!" Nayla exclaimed.

"Yes, a stud," Ming answered. "And, girl, she was fine!"

"Fine? What do you mean, fine? I thought you didn't do studs," Nayla laughed.

"I don't, but shit, that one that stopped to help me today has me thinking. I want to know what it's like. You feel me?" Ming leaned in to give Nayla a high five.

"Well, I say, do your thang girl. Did you get her number?" Nayla asked.

"No, hell, no. She left before I could. You see, she pulled up and asked if I needed some help. I told her no. I didn't want to be any bother and she replied it's no bother at all. So, girl, she took off her shirt and I damn near hit the ground."

"Took off her shirt for what?" Nayla squealed.

"She didn't want to get her shirt dirty," Ming replied. "But, girl, she smelled so damned good. She looked good and I am curious to know more. I have never had an interest in studs, but girl, oh, I would love to have her between my legs."

"Wow, Ming, are you serious? I can't believe you are talking about a stud like this."

"I know and I don't know where this feeling just came from. I wanted to ask her name. Before I could, the roadside assistance guy pulled up and pussy blocked," Ming said with a hint of frustration in her voice.

"Well, maybe, you will run into her again. Or, if not, now you can start dating studs or, at least, give them a chance."

"Maybe so, but I would like to have a conversation with her," Ming said wistfully. "But anyway, what about you? What are you going to do about your sister and when are you coming out the closet?"

"I don't know, Ming. I don't want to talk about that. Anyway, let's talk about something else, like who is this new client of yours that you are being so secretive about?"

"I told you at brunch. I didn't want to disclose it. So, stop asking. I am still thinking about studs right now!" Ming laughed.

"I won't breathe a word," Nayla said. "Just give me a little hint."

"If I told you, I would be forced to hurt you," Ming laughed.

"Okay, okay," Nayla sulked. "Don't tell me then, damn, I'm just your best friend who should know these things."

"Yes, you will know in due time. We have a meeting in the morning to go over the contract. We have been in talks for a few weeks and I hope to be hired as their attorney."

"Well, I hope you get it girl."

"So do I. Hey, let's go pick up something to eat. I need to lay it down early tonight."

"Okay," Nayla replied. "Let's go." She grabbed her things and she and Ming headed out of the door to grab a bite to eat.

DC went home thinking about her appointment for the next morning. She was meeting a new lawyer that had been highly recommended. *I hope she turns out to be everything they say she is,* she thought to herself.

When she arrived at home, DC immediately started to relax and unwind. But, she didn't want to get too comfortable, yet. She wanted to ensure that everything was ready so she didn't have to do anything in the morning. Just as she was getting her clothes together, her phone began to ring.

"Hello," DC answered.

"Hey, man. What's up? What's going on?" the caller asked.

"Nothing much," DC said. "Just getting ready for the business meeting tomorrow. What's up with you?"

"Just getting in," the voice on the other end of the phone responded.

"Oh, I thought you would have been home by now," DC said.

"I would have, but on my way home, I stopped to help a woman with a flat tire that was stranded. I must add that she was so beautiful, just beautiful. She was dressed in workout gear, but DC, man, she looked good and smelled good, too."

"Smelled good? I'm scared to ask, was she coming back from or headed to the gym?" DC said while laughing.

"Ha, ha, you got jokes. No, smart ass, she was on her way to the gym when her car caught a flat. I offered to help and she said yes. Even if she wasn't beautiful, I would have stopped to help. But, man, I wish I would have gotten her number or even given her my card."

"Why didn't you?" DC asked.

"Shit, I was going to, but the roadside assistance guy showed up and put a monkey wrench in my program."

"I'm sorry, man," DC replied. "Better luck next time. There are other beautiful women here in the city. I will have to take you to Dashes with me and my stud buddies the next time we go. That place is filled with fine ass women. You will be able to find you someone there."

"Okay, that's cool. So, call me once you're done with your meeting, tomorrow."

"Okay, will do. Talk with you later." DC replied.

"Okay, talk to you later. Bye."

Just as she was getting out of the shower, PG's cell phone rang. "Hello."

"Hi," the voice on the other end said. "It's Mia. Are we still on for tonight?"

"For sure," PG said. "So tell me, girl, what do you have in mind?"

"Whatever you like, I'm down for," Mia replied.

"Oh, I like to hear that," PG said. "So, what's the address so that I can come on over and we can get this started?"

"My address is 4210 South Summit. It's bell number 3."

"Okay, give me a minute to finish getting dressed and I'm on my way."

"Cool, I'll see you when you get here."

"Keep it wet for me," PG said as the two hung up the phone.

Once PG was done getting dressed, she glanced around the room to make sure she had everything that she needed. She looked inside her bag. *All good*, she thought. With that, she headed out of the door with her overnight bag to put it down on Mia.

PG arrived at Mia's place and rang bell number 3.

"Who is it?"

"It's PG."

"Okay," Mia said and buzzed her in.

As PG made her way up the stairs, she couldn't wait to put it down on Mia. As PG approached Mia's apartment, she could see her standing in her doorway. Mia was wearing nothing but a thong and a tee shirt that hung just past her breasts, exposing her abdomen.

"Hey there, come in. I have been waiting for you," she purred seductively.

"Damn," PG replied. "All that ass is for me?"

"Of course," Mia said.

"Oh, what did I do to deserve a greeting like this one?" she asked as she gave Mia a hug. *She's soft to the touch*, PG thinks.

Taking PG's hand into hers Mia, leads PG into the apartment and to the couch. "Sit down," she commands.

PG sat down with her legs spread wide enough for Mia to stand between them. PG drank Mia in with her eyes. She took notice of every womanly curve that Mia's body possessed.

"Your perfume smells so good," PG said to Mia.

"You look good," Mia responded.

The king of R&B was playing in the background. *There certainly was going to be a whole lot of kisses going on tonight*, thought PG as she hummed the words to the song. She then rested her hungry hands upon the sides of Mia's waist. PG slowly ran her hands down to Mia's hips, eyes focused on her eyes. They stared intensely at one another because they both knew what was about to transpire.

PG pulled Mia gently to the couch and began to softly kiss her lips, all the while still caressing her body. PG slowly began to remove Mia's t-shirt.

"Oh, shit," PG growled as her lust went up a degree higher as she sees Mia's lovely breasts bounce out free. Her nipples were already swollen and hard from arousal. PG's mouth had other plans now as her lips left Mia's soft lips to taste another part of her.

PG eased to the side of Mia's neck and sprinkled gentle kisses up and down it, as her lips retraced the path leading to Mia's earlobe. Gently, PG sucked on Mia's earlobe bringing her lips slightly up to softly whisper, "Damn, you're so sexy baby."

Mia angled for PG to lie back on the couch as she brought her body down to lie on top of her. They began to kiss again. PG's hands got demanding as she reached down to massage Mia's ass. Mia positioned herself so that her breasts were about an inch away from PG's mouth.

PG sucked Mia's nipple into her mouth and the sudden gesture made Mia moan. The sound of her moans made PG all the more eager to be inside of her. PG's thoughts turn to getting Mia completely out of her clothes, then fucking her nice and slow.

PG slid Mia's thong to the side and inserted her strap. Mia moaned loudly as the tip of the strap penetrated her wet throbbing pussy.

"It's ok, baby," PG whispered in her ear. "I won't hurt you."

Mia slid up and down PG's strap. With every move, PG slid deeper and deeper into Mia's tight pussy.

"Yes, baby, like that," PG exclaimed to Mia as she moved up and down giving PG full access to her wetness.

CHAPTER FOUR

Today is the day, thought Ming as she arose from her night of slumber. "Thank you, heavenly father, for this day," she said aloud as she sat up in her bed.

Let's get it started, she thought. *Today, I must impress DC with my skills so that she will hire me as her attorney.*

With that thought, Ming went to her closet to pick out something to wear to work. *Perfect*, she thought as she picked out a three-piece skirt set with wrap up the leg high heels. She laid the outfit on the bed then went to the bathroom to shower and get ready.

Ming checked herself thoroughly in the mirror. She wanted everything to be perfect and in its place from her hair to her teeth, to her jewelry, to her legs right down to her shoes. Ming was glad she decided to wear the open toe heels. The weatherman said it would be nice and sunny today. She didn't want to pass up a chance to show off her beautifully manicured toes.

After adding the finishing touches, Ming headed out of the door, briefcase in hand. She got into her car and decided on inspirational music for her drive to her office. She had some good old gospel music in her collection. *Praise Him in Advance* was the perfect one to play. She loaded the CD and sang her way to work.

When Ming arrived at her office, she noticed Angie's car in the parking lot. *Good she's in bright and early as I asked. That's why I love her,* she thought.

"Good morning, Ming," Angie smiled as Ming walked in the door.

"Good morning, Angie," replied Ming as she walked up to her desk.

"Don't you look good, today."

"Why, thank you," Ming smiled broadly. "I try. You're looking pretty good yourself. How was your evening last night?"

"Oh, it went well. I told her I had to get home in order to be here bright and early."

"Thank you, my friend and employee," Ming laughed as Angie joined in. "Oh, I need for you to prepare the conference room for me. Make sure the overhead projector is working. Also, call the corner bakery and have some breakfast pastries and donuts, along with some green tea, coffee, etc., sent over for my meeting this morning."

"Yes, will do," Angie answered as she picked up the phone to make the food arrangements.

Ming walked into her office and prepared for DC's arrival.

Meanwhile, across town, DC was also just waking up. She lay in her bed, in the condo that she was renting while in town, taking in the sunrays that were coming through the bedroom window.

"Oh, it's great to be home. I sure miss the Chi," she said aloud as she stretched. "And this view of downtown is spectacular!"

DC walked into the gourmet kitchen, put on a pot of water for a cup of green tea, and made herself an egg white omelet. While enjoying her breakfast, DC turned on the TV to check the weather for the day. Sunny and warm is the forecast. With that information, DC headed to the shower to get ready for the meeting with her new potential lawyer.

DC arrived at Ming's office right on time. She was a big fan of punctuality and didn't like to be late for anything, if possible. As DC walked into the office, Angie greeted her warmly.

"Good morning, may I help you?"

"Good morning, and yes, you may help me, beautiful. My name is Dominique Carter and I'm here to see Ms. La'Ming Foster."

"Just one moment, please," Angie said as she picked up the phone to call Ming.

"Ms. Foster, Ms. Dominique Carter is here to see you," she said when Ming answered.

"Thank you, Angie," Ming responded. "Can you please show her into the conference room?"

"Yes, I will," Angie said and hung up the telephone.

"Follow me, Ms. Carter," Angie said to DC. Angie lead the way into the conference room and asked, "Aren't you DC, the famous model?"

"Yes, I am," DC replied.

"I love your work," Angie said. "Welcome to Chicago and our offices."

"Thank you," DC responded as she walked into the conference room.

"Help yourself. There are coffee, tea, donuts and all kinds of goodies there for you to enjoy."

"Thank you, again," DC responded.

"You're welcome. Ms. Foster will be with you shortly."

Angie could not believe it. The new client that Ming was referring to was DC, the stud model. *My goodness was she gorgeous. I would love to get a piece of that apple*, Angie thought to herself as she walked back to her desk. She picked up the phone to call Rachael.

"Girl, what are you doing?"

"Putting on my clothes getting ready for work, why?"

"You will never guess who the new client Ming is trying to land is?" Just as Angie was getting ready to tell her, Ming walked pass Angie's desk. "Hold on," Angie whispered into the phone.

"Sshh, be quiet," Ming said. "Not yet, don't say anything."

"Too late," Angie said. "You should have told me that's who the client was going to be."

"This is why I didn't tell you, big mouth. Who are you talking to?"

"Rachael, she won't say anything."

Ming just rolled her eyes and went on to meet DC in the conference room.

"Girl, its DC," Angie exclaimed as she returned to the phone conversation. "DC, the model!"

"Really? How does she look in person?" Rachael asked.

"Fine, fine, fine," Angie said. "You should come over here before you go to work."

"Okay, girl, I am on my way. I have to see her."

Rachael hung up and thought to herself, *oh, oh, oh, a potential RL. Yes, she has it all: the look, the money, the glamour, the fame and the means. Just what I need*, Rachael says to herself. *I am going to have to make myself extra, extra sexy and glamorous. I know*, thinks Rachael, *I'll wear the form fitting wrap dress with a garter and thigh high stockings. That will surely turn her on.*

Rachael dressed with only one thing on her mind. How much she could get from DC and how far would she have to go to get it. Normally, it wouldn't take much for her to get the things that she wanted. Some women are very generous when they are in the company of a beautiful lady. But for DC, she wouldn't mind doing a little bit extra. Hell, that girl was fine and, if anyone could get her attention while she was here, Rachael could.

When Rachael arrived at Ming's office, she looked at herself one last time in her mirror to check her appearance. Make up, check. Everything was perfect.

"Let's go and let the party begin," she said aloud.

Rachael made her way out of her Lexus ISF and up the walkway to Ming's office. Her walk was on point. Her hips were swaying ever so slightly with every step so that her dress showed off her thigh high stockings. It gave such a pretty picture to her shapely thighs.

"Thank you for this opportunity to pitch to you how beneficial my services could be to you if you were to become my client. It has been wonderful meeting you, as well," Ming said to DC while they made their way to the front of Ming's office complex.

"It has been a pleasure to meet you, as well, and I am very impressed with your quality of work, as well as, your record of accomplishment. You shall be hearing from me very soon."

"I look forward to your decision," Ming said to DC as she reached out to shake her hand.

Just as they were saying their goodbyes, Rachael walked in. *Wow, she is stunning*, DC thought to herself.

"Good morning," Rachael said to Ming and DC as she entered the front office where they were standing.

"Good morning," Ming responded to Rachael. Ming then turned to DC. "DC, allow me to introduce my good friend, Rachael Wilson."

Rachael extended her hand to DC and said, "Please to meet you."

DC smiled, "No, the pleasure is all mine. Nice to meet you."

Ming then turned to Angie, "Please show Ms. Wilson to my office."

On that cue, Angie and Rachael disappeared around the corner to Ming's office.

"Well," Ming said as she continued to walk DC to the door. "Thank you, once again, for the opportunity to meet with you. Take care and have a wonderful rest of the day."

"You, as well," DC replied. "I will be contacting you ASAP with my decision."

"I look forward to it," Ming replied as DC turned and walked out of the door.

In Ming's office, Rachael and Angie were talking about how fine DC was when Ming walked in.

"What the hell, you guys? This is my place of business. What are you doing here Rachael?" Ming asked. "You called her and told her to come up here didn't you, Angie?" she scolded.

"Well, yeah. How could you keep a client like DC under wraps like that?" Angie asked.

"Because, first, I need to get her as a client before I have you damned groupies all over her," Ming said.

"Well, I would love to be a groupie for her. Oh yeah," Angie said.

"Get your slimy thoughts off that one," Rachael said. "She's mine."

"Wait a minute, you two, DC doesn't want either one of you heifers," Ming laughed.

"Whatever," they both said at the same time.

"So when will you know if she is going to hire you," Angie asked.

"No. When will you be able to introduce us once again and I can then work my magic?" Rachel asked.

"You know what? You need to get out of my office and go to work, Rachael, and you need to get back to work, Angie."

"Okay, okay," they both said in unison as they exited Ming's office.

"Hey, come with me to the conference room," Angie told Rachael. "There are some treats in there left over from her meeting with DC. I am going to pass them out in the office. You want some?"

"Sure," replied Rachael. "Where did you all get them from? You know I don't just eat anything."

"Girl, we got them from the bakery around the corner," replied Angie.

Rachael tasted a pastry and scrunched up her face. "Yuck, no baby, don't patronize that bakery anymore. I know a caterer who is a hundred times better. We use her at the hotel all the time. I will forward you her info."

"Cool," Angie said. "Well, I better get back to work before boss lady has my ass and not in the way I would like."

"Girl, you crazy. I'll send you that info and I will see you later," Rachael said as she hugged Angie goodbye. Rachel went out of the door to get to work.

DC thought about Miss Rachael Wilson when she left the meeting with Ms. Foster. *I would like to take her on a date*, thought DC. *Maybe, just maybe.* DC picked up the phone and called her business manager, Kimoni.

"Hello?"

"Hey, what's up?" DC said to Kimoni when she picked up the phone.

"Nothing much," Kimoni responded.

"How did your meeting with the new attorney go?"

"Man, it went great. How about you meet me for a late breakfast, early lunch?"

"You know they have a name for that," Kimoni snickered. "It's called brunch."

"Well, brunch is for femmes. So, let's just meet to eat. How about that?"

"Cool. Where would you like to meet?" Kimoni asked.

"How about Delish? It's right off of canal. Do you know where it is?"

"Yeah," replied Kimoni. "I will see you there in about thirty minutes."

"Ok, cool, see you then," DC said then disconnected the call.

CHAPTER FIVE

Both Kimoni and DC arrived at Delish at the same time. They greeted each other as they walked up to the entrance of the café. Once inside, they spotted a nice, cozy, private spot in the back.

Kimoni turned to DC and said, "Hey you go get the seats and I'll order us something to eat. I don't want you to be recognized and we won't be able to talk."

"Ok," DC said. "I just want something to drink."

DC headed towards the spot at the back of the café to sit down. While waiting for Kimoni to return DC, thought about the beautiful woman she had just met at Ms. Foster's office. *Rachael,* she said her name to herself. She was breathtaking. *I wonder would she be willing to go out with me.*

"DC! DC!" Kimoni calling her name snapped her out of her daydream. "Hey, what kind of drink do you want?"

"Oh, get me an iced tea please," she said.

"Will do. I'll be right back."

Upon returning with the food and drinks, Kimoni asked DC, "Hey man, what were you daydreaming about a minute ago?"

"Man, when I was leaving the attorney's office, one of her friends walked in and I have to say, she was hot. I was just thinking that I would like to take her out while I'm in town."

"Oh, that's cool. So, what was her name," Kimoni asked.

"Rachael," DC answered.

"Well, at least you know where to find the woman you are interested in and you got a name. My mystery woman, I don't know who she was. But that's over and done, even though I would love to take her out and get to know her. You know what I mean?"

"Yeah, I do," said DC.
"So, tell me about your meeting with the lawyer."

"It went very well, I must say. She has a very good track record, her business sense is on point and I love her ethics. Overall, it seems like she has every great quality that I need in an attorney. Not to mention her rates are great. Also, she seems to really enjoy her job and it's not about the money, in any way. I really like that. I got a good vibe that she will work hard and diligently to get me the best and nothing less."

"That's good, then," replied Kimoni. "If you feel that strong about her and her work, then you should give her a try. If you decide to do so, then that means I need to meet up with her as soon as possible."

"I will need to give her a tutorial of your schedule and the things that you will need right away."

"Most def. I will sleep on it tonight and let both you and her know in the morning."

"Sounds good. So, what about the pretty lady you met in her office today?"

"Don't know. I don't want to come on too strong, but she is definitely someone I would like to spend time with," answered DC.

"I wish I had gotten Ms. Ladies number. She was someone I would have loved to get to know. But, hey, it's a lot of beautiful ladies in this wonderful city. I will come across someone."

"For sure, Kimoni, for sure," said DC as the two friends finished with their lunch.

Rachael arrived at her office with DC still on the brain. *Oh, I need to try to meet up with DC on my own time and turf. But, how*, she thought. Rachael remembered that she needed to send Angie the caterer's information so that she could get some real food up in that office. She laughed to herself as she flipped through her contact rolodex on her desk. She found the number for Shar Hill.

The hotel had been using Shar's services for a while, she was a very good cook. All of the dishes that she sent were exceptional, so why not pass on the work to her. She owned her own business and she was family. Not family as in kin, but family as a lesbian and this is a sister hood. We try to stick together as much as we can. Rachael picked up the phone to call Angie to give her the information.

"Hi, Angie, it's me, Rachael. Here is the number for the caterer I told you about this morning. It's (312) 763-0005. Her name is Shar Hill."

"Okay, hon, have a good one. Call me later so you can meet me so we can hang out tonight."

"Okay, love ya, bye."

Rachael hung up the phone. *Let me get on with my day*, she thought.

Back at Ming's office, Ming was at her desk thinking that she had a very good chance of DC hiring her as her lawyer. Ming picked up the phone to call Nayla to let her know who the mystery client was since Angie had already let the cat out of the bag.

"Hello," Nayla answered in a sleepy voice.

"Rise and shine, my love," Ming tells her. "It's time to get up. The day is passing you by."

"What time is it?" Nayla asks.

"It is a little passed noon," Ming answered.

"Oh," Nayla yawns. "So, what's up? Still thinking about the stud that helped you on the side of the road?" laughed Nayla.

"Well, yes and no. I called you because I wanted to tell you who my new secret client is, well was. Angie has already opened her big mouth and told Rachael. I wanted to tell you all together once it became official. I don't know yet if she is going to hire my firm, but it's Dominique Carter."

"DC the model," Nayla exclaimed as she sat up in her bed. "Get the fuck out of here! Oh baby, I'm happy for you. She is fine. Oh, I hope she hires you on. Wow, she is really famous among the LGBT community. When will you know if she is going to elect to use your services?"

"I'm not sure. Hopefully, by the end of the week."

"Well, when you get it, because I know you will, I will do an article on DC, maybe an exclusive. Just let me know and I will work out the details."

"Why, thank you, Nayla. Thank you for having such faith in me and I will certainly let you know the outcome."

"That's what friends are for, Ming. So what's on your agenda for today?"

"Nothing much, really. Just tying up some loose ends here. I wanted to go out and have a cocktail to try to loosen up and get that stud off of my mind."

"Oh, you are still thinking about her?"

"Yes, I am and it's crazy. I even was checking DC out. Not in a way to get with her, but just her stud swagger."

"Well, I know this cool spot that has poetry sets on Mondays. We can check it out if you like," Nayla said.

"Sure. What time should I be ready?"

"Umm, you can pick me up around 7:30 that way we can get a good seat."

"Sounds good. I will be at your place at 7:30, then."

"Okay, boo. See you then."

"Bye," said Ming and she hung up the phone.

Nayla arose from her bed to start on her day, well what was left of it. *Thank goodness for the ability to work from home*, she thought. She got out of the bed with a few things on her mind. The first being how she would write a piece about DC. She had always admired her courage and strength, being a stud model.

The other is what was she going to do about what her sister saw. It had been weighing heavy on her that she lied, but she didn't know what else to do. Deep down she knew that she would have to face the music one day and face facts that she was, indeed, a lesbian in every sense of the word.

But, in the meantime, she wasn't ready for the world to know. *Why should she? What she did in the privacy of her own bedroom was her business and her business alone. Why should anyone else care that she loved every inch of a woman from the way they smelled down to the way they tasted. Whose business is it that she loves to eat pussy?* That should only matter to the person she's entertaining in her bedroom.

But, that's not the world we live in. People are always in your business judging you, what you do, and who you do. It's already hard being a black woman, but to add gay, black woman, it gets even harder. Most straight women think that you want them or you are checking them out, which can't be any further from the truth. The truth be told is those straight women want a taste and don't know how to get it. *I should know. That was me once*, thought Nayla. *That is until I had my first lesbian experience.*

It seems like it was just yesterday when she met the woman that would change her life forever. While in the bookstore around the corner from her apartment, Nayla was in the LGBT section trying to find something that would give her some answers to the feelings she had been having. She hadn't given in, fully, to the attraction she had been feeling towards women. She was flipping through a book titled, *How To Tell If You're A Lesbian*. She was excited about the book because maybe it would give her some insight on what she knew all along, but didn't want to admit to herself: she was gay.

While deep in her thoughts, she heard someone say, "Great book, but only you can say whether or not you're gay."

Nayla looked up to see a breathtaking woman standing in front of her.

"Hi, my name is Kimberly Brooks, but you can call me Kim, for short," she said as she extended her hand to shake Nayla's.

"Hello, I'm Nayla, Nayla Ivy," she replied as she extended her hand in response. Nayla dropped the book and her papers. "Oh, clumsy me," Nayla said as she bent down to get the book and all her papers.

"Let me help," Kim replied.

Kim slowly bent down to help Nayla with the mess she had just created. Nayla couldn't help but be drawn into her delightful smell. With every breath she took, she tried to inhale as much of Kim as she possibly could. Once they collected all of the papers, Kim couldn't help herself.

She asked, "Why do you need a book to tell you if you like pussy or not?"

Stunned by the question Nayla was at a loss for words. She was already nervous and that question didn't make it any better.

"Hey, come have dinner with me and we can talk over why you really have this book."

Kim took Nayla by the hand and the next thing she knew they were walking out of the door. For her, that's when it all started. Nayla wanted to be with Kim, all of the time. She just couldn't get enough of her. Kim knew she wanted Nayla just as much as Nayla wanted her.

For Kim, she would condition Nayla, get her out her shell, and while doing it, bang the fuck out of her. You see, Nayla was new fish, never been tampered with, and Kim loved it. Kim knew once she ate that pussy, Nayla would never go back to men, so she thought.

Nayla had different plans. You see, she loved this newfound relationship, but she wasn't ready for the world to know. Every moment that she could spend with Kim, she did. But, as they grew closer, Kim wanted more than Nayla could give.

One day after they had made love endlessly, Kim turned to Nayla and said, "You know I love you right?"

"Yes," responded Nayla. "I love you, too."

"No," said Kim. "I am falling in love with you and I want so much more. Move in with me. Be mine and only mine."

"What do you mean, Kim?"

"I want you to be my woman and we be together as a couple and stop all this sneaking around shit. No more pretending I'm just your friend. I want everyone to know I am more than just that."

"Why does everyone have to know? What we have going is good. Why do we have to?"

"No," said Kim before Nayla could finish. "Yes, what we share is good, but I am not going to continue to live a lie. Watch you smile in guys' faces or lie to your family about who I am. I can't take it anymore," Kim said as she started to cry. "Please, baby," pleaded Kim. "Let me take care of you, take care of us. I promise it will be wonderful. Just give our love a chance. You will see."

"I don't know, baby. I can't," Nayla said shaking her head as she started to cry.

"Don't cry, baby," Kim said as she kissed the tears running down Nayla's face. "I will protect you. I promise."

CHAPTER SIX

The phone ringing snapped Nayla out of her daydream. "Hello," she said.

"Hey, it's me. I was calling you back to find out what is the name of the place where we are going tonight," Ming said.

"It's called the Sound Board," replied Nayla.

"Okay, I will see you later on tonight, bye."

"Ok, bye," replied Nayla and she hung up the phone. Reminiscing about her old love made her give her a call. Even though she and Kim didn't work out, they still remained friends, which was something Nayla was truly grateful for.

"Hey, this is K. What can I do for you today?"

"Hello, Kim. This is Nayla. How are you?"

"I know who you are Lala. How are you?"

Lala was the name Kim used to call her when they were together. "I'm good. I want to see you, if that's okay?"

"Sure, I'm on my way to the station. How about you meet me there?"

"No problem. I will see you in a minute."

"Ok," Kim said and the two hung up the phone.

Nayla jumped in the shower, got dressed and she was off to meet Kim.

~

Kim was a DJ for WLRE radio. She was the host of the show, Radio Talk 2Nite. She and Nayla had a complicated relationship years ago. Once she saw that Nayla couldn't give her what she wanted and needed, the two split. She will always love Nayla, but she couldn't live the closet life with her. She hoped that one day Nayla would find the courage and the strength to face who she really was. It was hard walking away from her, but she didn't have any regrets.

Kim's forum at work consisted of interviewing famous and not so famous people along with playing music. The interviews were the bulk of the segments.

Kim wasn't surprised that Nayla called. She would call from time to time when she had that itch that she wanted to be scratched. Kim didn't mind doing just that in the beginning. But now, that's a no go. She didn't do bi chicks that were in the closet. What she shared with Nayla was in her past and she planned on keeping it there.

"Hey, ya'll," she waved to the radio crew as she entered the studio.

"You are always super early," one of the interns said as she walked by.

"Take note, my dear, so you can one day be where I am and that's head DJ," Kim responded with a smile.

Kim entered into the small room that she called an office. She was looking over her notes to see what the agenda was for her show tonight. Her producer hadn't made it in yet to go over the show's format.

Kim was looking through the paperwork of the current advertisers on her show. This is one of the ways she stayed on top of what was going on, what was hot and what was not. She looked up as she heard a knock at the door and saw Nayla enter her office.

"Hey you," Nayla said as she walked into Kim's tiny office.

"Hello there, you, and what do I owe the honor of this visit," Kim asked smiling broadly.

"Oh, nothing much. I was thinking about you today and I just wanted to touch base to see how you were doing."

"I'm fine," Kim replied. "Just working hard, that's all. You know me."

"Yes, I do," Nayla said smiling knowingly. "So, what's going on with you besides work?"

"What? Are you asking about who I'm fucking now?" Kim responded, shocked.

"No, no, that's none of my business, but since you brought it up, who ARE you fucking now?"

"NOYDB," replied Kim.

"Now, what the hell does that mean?" Nayla asked.

"It means none of your damned business." They both started to laugh.

"Oh, you got jokes now I see," Nayla said.

"You already know how I get down, don't act like you have forgotten." Kim said with a smile.

"You are something else. Hey, I have a question. Would you do an interview for me as a favor?" asked Nayla.

"Depends. Who is the person?" Kim asked.

"Well, I can't disclose that right now because the details aren't worked out yet. But, just know the person is famous, and if you do this for me, I will do a piece in the magazine for you."

"Well, I don't need a piece in the magazine, but tell you what," Kim said. "I was just looking through the businesses that advertise on my show. I ran across a store that is owned by family. How about you do an article on that store?"

"Sure, if you like, I will do that," said Nayla.

"Well, let me get in contact with the business owner and see if she would like to do an article."

"I don't see why she wouldn't. It's free."

"Yeah, that's true, but some people can be funny acting," Kim said.

"True, true, I agree."

"Well, I will get back to you on what she said if it's a yea or a nay."

"Okay, cool. I will let you know, soon, about that interview. I should find something out tonight."

"Okay. Will do."

"Alright, Kim," Nayla said as she headed for the door. "I will see you later, so you can get back to work."

"For sure," Kim said standing. "It's almost time for me to go on the air."

Nayla left Kim's office and headed back home. She had to get ready to go out with Ming later that evening.

DC decided to go ahead and hire Ms. Foster as her attorney. She didn't want to wait until the next day to let her know. She picked up the phone and called Ms. Foster's office.

"Thank you for calling the Law Offices of La'Ming Foster. This is Angie. How may I help you?"

"Good afternoon, Angie, this is Dominique Carter. Can I speak to Ms. Foster, please?"

"Why yes," Angie answered. "Just one moment, please."

Angie called into Ming's office. "Hey, Ming. Dominique Carter is on line one."

"Put her through. Thanks, Angie," Ming said. Once she heard the connection indicating that DC was now on her line, Ming announced, "This is Ms. Foster. Hi, how are you, Ms Carter?"

"I'm good," responded DC. "I wanted to call and let you know I am electing to hire you as my attorney."

"Thank you, DC. Rest assured that I will work extremely hard for you and give you the best representation that you deserve."

84

"I know you will, Ms. Foster. That is why I am choosing you. I would like to set up a team meeting so that I can introduce you to my business manager, as soon as possible."

"Sure. How about Wednesday afternoon at 1:30 pm at my office?" Ming asked.

"That should be fine. Just let me check with my manager to make sure her schedule is clear. I will get back to you soon. Is that okay?"

"Yes, that is fine. You can speak with me directly or leave a message with my secretary, Angie."

"Will do. So, if all is clear, I will see you on Wednesday at 1:30 pm."

"See you then. Have a great rest of the day. Thank you once again, Ms. Carter. I won't let you down."

"Have a great evening," DC replied then hung up the phone.

~

Ming blew out a big sigh of relief as she rested the handset in the cradle of the telephone. "Angie,

85

can you come into my office and shut the door, please?"

Angie walked into Ming's office closing the door behind her. "What's up, boss lady?" she inquired.

"Hey, I got it! I got DC as a client!" she squealed.

They immediately started dancing excitedly in front of Ming's desk.

"Hey, go out with me so we can celebrate. Nayla and I are going to a place called the Sound Board, tonight. Call Rachael and you guys meet us there at 7:30 pm.

"Okay," Angie said. "Sounds good."

"Hey, take the rest of the day off. I will see you tonight."

"Okay," Angie said smiling from ear to ear. Angie left the office to go call Rachael. Rachael didn't answer so she left a message on her voicemail.

"Hey girl. She got DC as a client. We're going out to celebrate. Call me when you get this message."

When DC hung up with Ming, she called Kimoni to tell her that she decided to hire Ms. Foster as her attorney. She ended up having to leave a message because Kimoni didn't answer her phone. Just as soon as she hung up the phone from leaving the message, DC's phone rang. It was PG.

"Hey, man. What's up? What you doing?" PG inquired.

"Nothing much. What about you?" DC replied.

"Was trying to find somewhere to watch a little T&A."

"T&A? What's that, a new show or something?"

"Not unless she will let you film them," PG chuckled. "T&A is titties and ass, man." They both fell out laughing.

"Man, you crazy as hell," DC said still laughing.

"I know. I know. If you're not doing anything, you should stop by Stony's place. We are going to get together and maybe play some videogames. She's trying out some new dishes and using us as her damn taste testers."

"Okay, cool, give me the address and I am on my way."

~

Everyone was at Stony's place. PG was playing Ray on the Xbox when DC walked through the door.

"Hey, what's going on ya'll," DC said as she walked in.

"Nothing much." Ray responded.

"You got it." Said PG.

"Oh, I can't call it, but I know it's good," she responded cheerfully. DC walked into the kitchen where Stony was preparing an awesome smelling meal.

"Hey, what's up man? Nice kitchen you got here," she said to Stony.

"Thanks, man. Cooking is my life so I have to keep it nice. Hey, taste this sauce and tell me what you think."

DC took a taste of the sauce. It was good. "Hey man, that's great."

"Thanks," Stony beamed, "help yourself to whatever you want to drink."

DC went straight to the fridge, grabbed a cold beer, and then went into the living room with the others.

While the others played Xbox, Stony created some great dishes for them to sample for her next catering job.

"DC, man, tell us again how is it to have so much pussy at your fingertips?" Ray prompted.

"It's great in the beginning, then you get tired of the different lady, different city thing. Then, it turns into is she really here for me or what I have to offer her."

"I hear that," Stony said as she walked into the living room from the kitchen. "You never can tell if they are genuine when you are a celebrity. They always show their true colors."

"All in all, you get to have anyone you like, however you like, because some of them are willing to do anything to be with you."

"Anything," repeated PG, "man, I am in the wrong business. I need to be a model. Hey, DC, hook me up so I can be down."

"It's not all glitz and glamour either. It's hard work. Up all hours of the day and night, different cities. You have to want this to service this."

"I hear you," Ray said as she gave DC some dap. "Now, come on down here so I can kick your famous ass in this football game."

"Bring it on," DC challenged. "Let the ass kicking begin."

The friends talked and played video games into the wee hours of the morning.

Ming went home to shower and change before her night of celebrating the acquisition of her new client.

She arrived at Nayla's house right on time. She rang the doorbell and waited patiently for Nayla to respond.

"Greetings," Nayla said as she flung open the door.

"Hey, Boo! Guess what? I got the job," Ming gushed.

"I told you. I knew you would. That is great news for you, Ming. I am so proud of you."

"Thanks, girl. Come on so we can get our drink on a little and enjoy some poetry." With that, they left to meet up with their other best friends.

~

Just as Nayla had said, the Sound Board was popping. It had a very good crowd for it to be a Monday night. Rachael and Angie arrived shortly after Ming and Nayla got to their seats. They both offered their congratulations to Ming as they gave her a big hug.

"Thank you, my sistas. Thank you," she beamed. "Come, sit down and order your drinks. They are on me tonight."

They ordered drinks and chatted about the day's events. They were so happy to celebrate Ming and her new client. Right before they could get deep into a conversation, the lights went dim. The emcee stepped on stage and introduced the poet for the evening. Her name was Lyric.

"Good evening, ladies and gentlemen. I am Lyric and this is my poem called Why…"

Games why do u play them
Lies why must you tell them
Why
Unfaithful that's who you are
A traitor that's who you've become
Why
Controlling in all aspects
Mean to the core
Why
Grow up I've moved on
I have someone who
Doesn't play games
Don't tell me lies
Has never been unfaithful
Wouldn't trade me for the world
We are equal and has nothing but
love for me
So don't ask me
Why

Lyric continued her set. This chick was hot. After drinking and listening to some good poetry, Ming didn't want to call it a night, but she had a busy day tomorrow. She now had to prepare for her official client.

Angie raised her glass and said, "Okay ladies, this is the last drink for the night. Let's toast our good friend on a job well done."

"Here, here," said Rachael.

"I second that notion," chimed in Nayla as they raised their glasses in toast to their friend.

CHAPTER SEVEN

When Angie got into work that morning, she called the caterer that Rachael recommended.

"Taste The Rainbow Catering Services, how may I help you?"

"Good morning," Angie said. "I need to speak with someone about placing an order to be delivered at one o'clock tomorrow. Your number was given to me by a friend who recommended that we try your services."

"Well that would be me," Stony replied. "What would you like to order?"

"I would like to place an order for 20 sub sandwiches along with a veggie/fruit tray. I would also like you to send 20 small bags of potato chips. You can do any flavors you like. Now for the sandwiches, I would like five ham, five turkey, five roast beef, and the last five, surprise me. For the condiments, please include Italian dressing, mustard, mayo, hot peppers, banana peppers, etcetera. For the drinks, please send five bottle waters, five ice teas, and ten bottles of soda pop. Again, you can mix and match those to your preference."

"Well, okay, I will certainly do my best," Stony replied.

"Thank you. I look forward to tasting your work."

"Does that complete your order?" Stony asked.

"Yes, it does. What is the total amount?" Angie asked.

"Let me calculate real fast. That will be one hundred and ninety five dollars. The price includes tax and delivery charges. What is the location for the delivery and how will you be paying for this today?"

"By credit card and the location is 521 Canal Street. We are across from the old Merrill Lynch building."

"Okay, great. I know exactly where that is. Thank you for your business," Stony said. "It is greatly appreciated. Please give me the name of who referred you so I can thank them."

"Not a problem, it was Rachael Wilson. Angie said before she hung up.

While on her way to work, Nayla picked up her cell and called Kim. Kim picked up immediately.

"It is the one and only, what can I do for you?"

"Hey, Kim, I have the details on the interview for you."

"Okay, okay, do tell," Kim responded.

"Well the person that you will be interviewing is DC."

"DC, the stud model?" Kim quizzed.

"Yes," Nayla replied.

"Wow, that's hella cool."

"I know, right?" said Nayla, "I just wanted to call you to let you know. Once you get to work today and you look at your time schedule, you can let me know what would be a good day for the interview."

"Yeah, no problem, Lala. Good looking out. Having DC on will send the ratings through the roof.

"I know, right? Now don't forget to call the person you picked for me to do the story on. Once you have confirmed with them that it's okay, send me a text with her information."

"Will do and thanks again for this."

"No problem," Nayla replied. "I'll be in touch with you soon."

"Talk with you later," Kim replied and the two hung up.

~

Even though Kim didn't have to be at work for a few hours, she got up and got dressed. She wanted to speak to the store owner in person rather than make contact on the phone. Frames was the name of the store and the motto was "We cater to everyone's Frame. So, if you can't find it here, you won't find it."

This is a really nice store, Kim thought as she walked in and took a look around. The store did have everything you could think of. It was well put together and the staff was very friendly.

"Hi, welcome to Frames. May I help you?" a sales associate asked Kim as she made her way into the store.

"Yes, my name is Kimberly Brooks and I work for WLRE radio station. I am her to see a Ms. Glover."

"Yes, just a moment while I call her office," the sales associate said as she picked up the phone to call PG. "Hi, PG, there is a lady from the radio station here asking to speak to you," she said once PG answered.

"Okay, tell her I will be right out."

"Okay," replied the sales rep and hung up the telephone. "Ms. Glover will be right out to see you."

"Thank you," Kim replied.

PG came out of her office and to the front to see who, from the radio station, wanted to speak to her.

"Hi," PG said as she approached Kim, "I'm Ms. Glover."

"Pleased to meet you," Kim said as she extended her hand to shake PG's hand.

"Hey, I know you," exclaimed PG, "you're the DJ from radio Talk 2Nite."

"Yes, I am," replied Kim.

"Come on into my office so we can talk," PG said as she proceeded to the back of the store where her office was located.

"Pardon the dust back here. We are doing some remodeling so please be careful," PG advised.

"Okay," Kim said as she followed.

Kim walked by a stud working on the electrical wires in the ceiling. She couldn't help but notice the tattoos on the stud's arms. *Nice*, she thought to herself.

"Come on have a seat," PG said to Kim once they were in her office.

"Thank you," she replied. "I know you're wondering why I'm here. I'm her to offer you some additional advertisement at no cost to you. See, your store was randomly chosen to be featured in an article for Out and About magazine."

"Wow, really? Thank you so much. What do I need to do?" PG asked.

"You must sign a consent form, in order to be interviewed and the rest will be left up to the writer.

Her name is Nayla Ivy. She will be contacting you here at the store in a few days to set up an appointment with you. She will provide you with all of the details of the article.

"Thank you, again," PG beamed happily.

"No problem. It was a pleasure meeting you," Kim said as she rose from the chair to leave.

PG stood up and extended her hand to shake Kim's. "Let me walk you out."

"No need," Kim replied. "I can find it, thanks. Have a great rest of the day."

"I sure will," PG replied. "You just made my day."

As Kim was exiting the office, Ray was getting her tools together. As Ray rose, she and Kim made direct eye contact. Feeling like she had been caught staring, Kim commented on Ray's tattoos.

"I love your tats."

"Thank you. Would you like to see them up close?" she asked.

"Sure," Kim replied as she walked closer to Ray. Ray stretched her arms out for Kim to get a full view.

"Beautiful," Kim replied.

"So are you," Ray said.

"Why, thank you," Kim blushed as they stood there for a brief moment. "Oh, I must get going. Take care."

"You do the same," Ray said back to her as she watched Kim walk away.

As Kim walked away, she could feel the intensity of Ray's stare as she watched her every move.

Hm..., Ray thought. *PG sure knows she gets some good chicks.*

While Ray was standing there thinking about Kim, PG walked up.

"Hey, how's it coming along?" PG asked.

"Oh, it's cool. I'm almost done. Hey, man, who was that just leaving your office?"

"Yeah, I was just coming out here to tell you about that. Come into the office, man, so I can tell you. That was the DJ from the radio show, Talk 2Nite.

"Really? Baby girl looks good."

"Yeah, she was looking good, but she came by to tell me that the store has been randomly chosen to be featured in an article for the magazine, Out and About.

"Damn, man, look at you moving on up. I'm proud of you," Ray said as she shook PG's hand.

"Thanks, man. It's been hard work, but it's worth it. You have to work hard to succeed and that's what I'm trying to do. Be successful."

"Well, you're starting in the right direction with your store. I thought baby girl was one of yours."

"Naw, man. Whenever it's about business, it's about business. I don't shit where I eat."

"I hear you, man. I would like to get to know her."

~

Once Kim left, she thought about the stud she had just seen and how good she looked on the ladder doing her work. *Oh, I just love women,* she thought. *It didn't matter if they were femme or stud as long as they are well put together.* Kim could tell the stud on the ladder was well put together. It was something about the way she was working. She had this ooh wee about herself.

I should have gotten her name. It has been a long time since I been on a date. It was well over due. Maybe I would go back to the store one day in hopes of running into her again. Naw, she was doing work on the store. It looked like electrical work. I'll run into her again. I will never forget those tats. They were hot to death, Kim daydreamed.

~

Kimoni had missed DC's call last night. She was preoccupied with something or, well, someone, who just came up. She called DC back to see what was going on. DC answered on the second ring.

"Hello?"

"Hey, man, what's going on? I'm sorry I missed your call yesterday."

"No, it's cool. I know you have a life too. I just wanted to let you know that I decided to hire Ms. Foster as my attorney."

"Oh, man, that's great."

"Yeah, I know. I just went with my gut feeling. We both have to meet with her tomorrow afternoon at 1:30 if you are available. Are you available?"

"I should be," Kimoni answered. "Let me check my blackberry to make sure." After a brief pause, Kimoni said, "It seems like I'm all clear. Tomorrow is good."

"Here is the office information," DC started to say.

"No, wait, text it to me so that I can Mapquest it. I don't have any paper or a pen in front of me right now."

"Okay, man. I'll just see you tomorrow."

"Sounds good," Kimoni replied before the two hung up the phone.

CHAPTER EIGHT

Stony had arrived bright and early to prepare the sandwiches for the twelve o'clock delivery. She would have to remember to ask again who the person was that recommended her for this job. She liked to send something complimentary to the person or business that made the referral.

Word of mouth is the best advertisement and she wanted to let the people who referred her work know that she appreciated it dearly. As Stony put the finishing touches on the lunch order, she thought about how blessed she was to have a business that was doing okay in this economy.

She was going to do something to give back to the community. She would have to give some thought to what she would do. Maybe she would ask her friends for some input, as well.

Time was winding down and Stony wanted to make sure the food was perfect. It was now eleven thirty, time to load up the food, and make her delivery. She wanted to make sure she had enough time to set up, properly. Once the van was loaded, she was on her way to deliver the order.

Stony arrived at exactly 11:50. She went inside the building to find out where she needed to set up the food.

"Good afternoon, may I help you," Angie asked Stony as she was entering the building.

"Good afternoon to you. I am from Taste the Rainbow catering and I have your lunch delivery outside. Where should the food be placed?" Stony asked.

"Yes, it needs to be set up in the conference room. How about you go and start bringing in the food and I will show you where it goes."

"Sounds like a plan. I will be right back," Stony replied as she headed out of the door.

Damn, Angie thought as Stony walked out the door. *She fine than a muthafucka. I got to have that.*

Angie got up from behind her desk to hold the door open for Stony as she came back. Angie made sure she stood close enough for Stony to brush by her as she entered the door.

"Thank you, so much," Stony said as she walked passed Angie.

"This way to the conference room," Angie told Stony. "I'm sorry. I didn't get your name."

"It's Shar Hill."

"Pleased to meet you, Ms. Hill. I hope your food tastes as good as you look."

"Most definitely," Stony said. "It's even better."

"Well, in that case, I can't wait to have a taste," Angie said with a seductive look on her face.

"Well, just a moment and you will be able to have all you can eat," Stony replied.

"Oh, I like that. Fine and aggressive," Angie retorted slyly as she unlocked the conference room door. "You can set up in here. You can go back and forth. I will keep the door propped open for you to bring the rest of your items in."

"Thank you so much," Stony replied. "And, what's your name?"

"Oh, I'm Angie. I'll be at my desk if you need anything and I mean anything. Just let me know."

"I will, Ms. Angie. Thanks," Stony chuckled with a slight grin on her face.

Stony was so used to women pursuing her aggressively that it didn't even faze her at times. She just shook her head and laughed at what had just happened. Stony finished setting up the food and the beverages.

As she gave the area a once over, she was satisfied that everything looked great. All the drinks were cold and the sandwich platter was wrapped tightly. *Everything was right, perfect*, she thought as she turned off the light and closed the door.

Stony walked back up to Angie's desk. "Hello, Ms. Angie. Everything is set in the conference room. If there is anything else you may need, please don't hesitate to call. Here is my card," Stony reached into her pocket and handed Angie a business card.

"Taste The Rainbow. What a perfect name for your business," Angie said. "Do you mind if I have a taste?"

"You're something else. How are you going to be flirting with me while we're conducting business?" she asked as she leaned on the desk.

"Well, what better time than the present? Tomorrow is not promised and I like to live life to the fullest."

"Point taken," Stony said as she took a look at her watch. It was now 12:45. "Well, I have to get going," she told Angie, "other deliveries."

"Well, don't let anyone else have a taste before I do," Angie said as Stony walked away and out of the door.

Stony just smiled and nodded her head.

~

Kimoni checked her text message for the address that DC had sent so that she could Mapquest the directions. She didn't want to get lost. After printing up the directions, she headed out of the door. It was 1:00pm and she wanted to make sure she had enough driving time. Once in the car, she activated her blue tooth and called DC.

"Hello," DC replied. "What's up?"

"Hey, man. I'm out the door and on my way to the meeting."

"Me too, man. I am getting ready to walk out the door now so I will meet you there. You have the correct name and address, right?" DC asked.

"Yes, I have it. I will see you there. Do you want me to wait for you in the parking lot or should I just go in?" Kimoni inquired.

"If we don't pull up together, then yeah, man, wait for me and we can go in together."

"Okay, cool. I'll see you in a minute."

"Okay, bye."

~

Traffic was perfect. It should only take me twenty minutes to get to the law offices, Kimoni thought. Twenty minutes later, she reached her destination. She was getting ready to call DC when she pulled in next to her.

"Hey, man. What's up" Kimoni said as she got out of the car and the two shook hands.

"Nothing much," DC replied. "I just want to sign these papers so that this is taken care of and I won't have to worry any more about representation."

"Okay, man. Let's go. You lead the way since you've been here before."

DC led the way up the walkway and into the building. As she reached the front desk, she said, "Good afternoon, Angie."

"Good afternoon, Ms. Carter. How are you?"

"I'm fine and you."

"I'm good," replied Angie, "and whom do you have with you?"

"This is Kimoni Grey, my business manager."

"Pleased to meet you, Kimoni," said Angie as she extended her hand towards Kimoni.

"The pleasure is all mine," Kimoni said.

"Just one moment while I tell Ms. Foster that you are here," Angie said as she picked up the phone to call Ming.

"Ms. Foster, DC and her business manager are here."
"Can you please show them to the conference room directed Ming, I will be there shortly."

"Okay, I will," Angie said as she hung up from Ming.

Angie came from around her desk and beckoned to the two ladies. "Follow me, please. Beautiful weather we are having," Angie said.

"It sure is." Said Kimoni

"I am enjoying every minute of it." Responded DC.

Angie opened the conference room door and turned on the lights. She walked over to the table where the food and drinks were set up.

"Help yourself. Lunch is being provided. There are a variety of sandwiches and drinks for you both to enjoy. Ms. Foster will be with you shortly."

"Thank you," Kimoni and DC replied.

"You're welcome. Take care and have a wonderful rest of the day," Angie said before she left the room.

"She's nice and good-looking too," Kimoni said.

"Yeah, she is, but wait until you meet Ms. Foster. She is beautiful, also."

They fixed themselves a plate of food that had been provided for them then they took a seat at the round table. They were eating and talking when Ming walked in.

"Good afternoon," she said as she went over to greet DC and her business manager. To her surprise the handsome stranger whom she had been thinking about was sitting in her conference room.

"Good afternoon," DC replied.

Kimoni froze for a moment with a piece of her sandwich stuck on her lip when Ming walked in the room. She wiped her mouth before speaking.

"Hello there," she said as she stood up to shake Ming's hand. She couldn't believe it. The mystery woman that had been on her mind was DC's lawyer.

"Why, hello to you. How are you?" asked Ming.

"I'm good, but now, even better now that I found you," Kimoni replied.

"Do you two know each other?" DC quizzed.

"DC," Kimoni said. "This is the lady that I told you about. I helped fix her flat tire."

"Oh, wow!" DC exclaimed and turned to Ms. Foster and said, "small world."

"Yes, it is indeed a small world," she said then turned to Kimoni. "I wanted to ask you for your information, but you left so quickly. I figured you were in a hurry."

"Well, yes and no. You were busy with the roadside assistance guy so I just made myself scarce."

"Oh, I see. Well, my name is La'Ming Foster," Ming said as she held out her hand.

"I'm Kimoni Grey," she said as she took Ming's hand into hers. *So soft*, she thought.

"Pleased to meet you. Now, shall we begin?"

They got straight to business. They went over all aspects of DC's business. They began with DC signing the contract to hire Ming as her attorney. Then Kimoni brought Ming up to speed on all of the things that DC needed to have reviewed. When they were done, Kimoni found that she was very impressed with Ming overall. She was beautiful, intelligent and very professional.

"Well, now that we have, everything signed and sealed," Ming said with a laugh. "Let me take just a moment to welcome you to my firm. As I stated to you before, I will work very diligently for you. I will give you the best representation that I possibly can."

"Why, thank you," DC said. "That is why I hired you." They all started to laugh.

Ming then turned to Kimoni staring at her as if she could just take a bite. "Ms. Grey…"

"No. Please call me Kimoni," Kimoni interrupted while thinking she wanted to get to know this woman better.

"Okay, Kimoni. How about you let me take you out to dinner to thank you for fixing my flat tire?"

"Now, that won't be necessary," Kimoni replied.

"I insist. It's the least I can do to thank you for helping me out like that. I would have still been on the side of the road," Ming said laughing.

"Okay, well, instead of you taking me out to dinner, how about I fix you dinner at my condo this Friday? Say eight o'clock?"

"Are you sure?" Ming asked.

"Yes, positive," Kimoni replied.

"Okay, sounds good to me," Ming said.

"Okay, here is my business card," Kimoni said. "My cell number is on it. How about you give me a call tonight and we can work out the details?"

DC was just sitting back watching her business manager in action. She kept saying she wished she could meet the woman that she helped and here it is, full circle. The woman happened to be my lawyer. *Small world, indeed*, thought DC.

"Well, I guess that about finishes everything, right ladies?" DC inquired. She figured they must have forgotten she was in the room.

"Oh yes, DC, we are done. I will look over all of the items that Kimoni gave to me. If I have any questions, I will give you a call." Ming announced.

"Sounds like a plan." DC responded.

"I will show you out, then, so you can get back to your day," Ming smiled as she stood.

Ming escorted DC and Kimoni to front desk where they exchanged goodbyes before DC and Kimoni left.

Once outside, DC turned to Kimoni and said, "Man that was wild. Who knew the lady you met was Ms. Foster? That's fucking wild."

"Tell me about it," Kimoni said as they approached their cars. "Well now that I know who she is, I can let her know that I am interested in her and maybe she feels the same."

"Maybe so," DC said. "She agreed to have dinner with you so that's a start."

"Yeah, man it is. Well, let me go, I have some errands to run. I'll check you out later."

"Cool, just hit me on the hip. Peace out," DC responded as she got in her car then drove away.

Ming watched as the two chatted in front of their cars for a moment. There was no doubt they were talking about her. She picked up the phone and called Nayla. Nayla was the only one of her friends that knew about her flat tire adventure. Nayla's phone went to voice mail. *Shit, she would have to leave a message.*

"Hey, Nayla it's Ming. Call me ASAP, I have something to tell you that is going to flip your wig. Bye love," she said as she hung up the phone.

CHAPTER NINE

Nayla was on the phone with Kim getting the details regarding the store she was doing the article on when Ming called. She would have to call her back.

"Okay, Kim, I got it. Thanks. I will call you and let you know how things went once I'm done."

"Okay," replied Kim, "I will talk to you later."

Nayla was getting ready to call Ming back, but her phone rang distracting her.

"Hello," she said.

"Hi," the voice on the other end responded. "What's going on?"

"Nothing. What about you?" Nayla asked.

"Oh, I was going to come over to see you."

Nayla cut her sister off quickly, "I am on my way out the door. I have to do an interview for the magazine. I will call you once I make it home."

"Okay," her sister said sounding disappointed. "I will talk with you later then, bye."

"Bye," Nayla said as she hit end on her cell phone.

I wonder what she really wanted, Nayla thought. *She has really been trying to get over here lately. Oh well*, Nayla thought as she started to call Parker Glover. Kim had given her the number and address to the store.

"Hello, thank you for calling Frames."

"Hello there. My name is Nayla Ivy. Is a Ms. Glover available?"

"No, she isn't right now. She just stepped out for a moment. Would you like to leave a message?"

"Umm… let me ask you this. Is she gone for the day or will she be back?"

"She should be back within the next 30 minutes," the woman on the other end stated.

"Okay, in that case, I don't need to leave a message. I will just come by. Thank you so much," Nayla said and hung up the phone she then dialed Ming's number. She got Ming's voicemail. *Oh well*, she thought, *I will just call her later on tonight.*

Nayla arrived at the store about 15 minutes later. From the outside, it looked very nice. She couldn't wait to see what the inside looked like.

Once inside, she was very impressed with the interior, as well. Everything was arranged very nicely and in good order. She walked around the store just browsing. She saw a really cute top and a dress that she had to have. Why not take advantage while she was waiting for Ms. Glover to arrive to get in a little shopping.

"Hello, how are you doing? That's a very sexy dress and I am sure it would look great on you," a smooth sexy voice said to Nayla.

Nayla turned around to face a tall, mocha colored stud with the pearliest white teeth she has ever seen. This stud was fine with her perfectly lined dreadlocks pulled to the back. Oh, she was debonair.

"Why, thank you. I am fine how about you?" Nayla asked.

"Well, I'm good, but even better now that I met you."

"Met? Have we actually met?" Nayla asked in a playful way.

"Well, sure," replied the stranger. "I just said hello and you responded. That is meeting, correct?" she smiled seductively.

"If you say so," Nayla said as she laughed at the stranger.

"I would love to take you out when you wear that. How about this, I take you out to dinner and we get into a little something, something?"

"A little something, something?" asked Nayla. "Now what exactly would that be?"

"Whatever your heart's desire," the stranger said confidently. "You tell me, and you got it."

"Wow, just like that, huh? You don't know me like that, but you would give me whatever my heart desired?"

"That's why I'm trying to get to know you. Just give me a chance. You'll see. I will make it worth your while."

"I'm sure you will," Nayla said. "Will you excuse me for a moment? I need to try these garments on before I purchase them."

"Okay, sweetheart. Do you need me to help you with that the stranger asked? You know, zip up something or even unzip something else?" she said with a grin.

Nayla smiled and said, "No, thank you. I can handle it myself."

"Okay," said the stranger with a shrug. "I will be waiting right here for you to give me your number once you're done trying on that dress you will be wearing when I take you out to dinner."

Nayla just smiled and proceeded to walk to the fitting rooms to try on the dress and the blouse. While trying on the clothes, Nayla thought to herself about life, her life, and most importantly her life as a lesbian. Here was this fine, sexy ass stud coming on to her and while she was interested she, also was cautious because of what others may think. *Fuck it*, she thought to herself, *if she is still out there waiting for me, I am going to give her my number.*

Everything was a perfect fit so she decided to buy both items. By the time Nayla was done in the fitting room, the handsome stranger was gone.

Damn, she thought. *Oh well, let me make my purchases and take them to the car.* Nayla went to the counter to pay for her clothes.

"Hi," said the sales associate. "Did you find everything to your liking?"

"Yes," responded Nayla.

"Great. The total will be $80.25."

Nayla went into her purse and handed the associate a one hundred dollar bill. "I do have a question," Nayla said. "Is Ms. Glover in?"

"Yes she is," the associate said. "Is there something you need or I can help you with?"

"Oh, no. My name is Nayla Ivy and I am here from Out and About Magazine."

"Just one moment while I call her office," the associate said as she picked up the phone. "Ms. Glover, there is someone here from Out and About magazine to see you," she said into the phone.

"Yes, yes," PG said. "Can you bring her back to my office and have her take a seat until I get there. I was on my way to the stock room. I will be back shortly."

"Sure," the associate replied and hung up the phone. She turned to Nayla and said, "Here is your change. Ms. Glover will see you now. Follow me."

The associate walked Nayla to Ms. Glover's office. She opened the door and beckoned Nayla inside.

"Please have a seat. Ms. Glover will be back in just one moment."

"Okay, thanks," Nayla replied.

Nayla began to get her recorder and note pad ready for the interview when she heard footsteps from behind and a familiar voice say, "Hi, how are you? I'm Ms. Glover."

Nayla turned around to see the stud from a few moments ago that asked to take her out.

"Oh wow, it's you. Ms. Lady who had me waiting for her number. Now is this a coincidence," PG stated as she walked into her office and took a seat behind her desk.

"Yes, it is," Nayla said. "In my defense, if you would have been still waiting, I would have given you my number."

"I know, because I was determined to get it from you," PG said with a grin. "You know, I'm breaking my business rule of not mixing business with pleasure. But, it would be my pleasure to mix my business with you," PG said as she reached out and took Nayla's hand into hers.

"You are too much, Ms. Glover," Nayla blushed.

"No, please call me PG. Now, before we conduct this interview, are you going to give me your number so I won't have to worry about that?"

"Yes," Nayla said. "I would have had to give you my number anyway."

"Okay, point taken. Let's get started then."

With that, Nayla conducted her interview for the magazine article. They chatted until Nayla was satisfied that she had enough material for her article.

"Well, Ms. Glover, oh, I mean PG, I'm done. If I have any other questions that I need answered, I will contact you." "I would also like to come back and have some pictures taken of you and the store to give a more visual effect."

"That's no problem. Whatever you need from me, or for me to do, I will take care of it."

"Thank you," Nayla said as she extended her hand for PG to shake.

"You're quite welcome," PG replied as they both stood up. PG kissed Nayla on the hand instead of shaking it. "Come on, beautiful, let me walk you out. Then we can talk details about our date and how soon it will be."

"Really," Nayla began as they exited PG's office. "You have a beautiful store here and I love the décor."

"Thanks."

"Now, I have one last question," Nayla said. "How do you know that I am in the life? I could be straight."

"That could be true," PG said, "but, if so, I am interested and I see you are too. And, you won't be straight for long," she said with a grin.

"So when we have our first dinner date, we can talk about you being straight or gay."

"You are too much," Nayla chuckled over her shoulder as she turned to leave.

"Perfect," PG said as she watched Nayla get in her car and leave.

Man it's something special about her I think I may keep her around for a while, she thought. The ringing of her cell phone took her out of her thoughts.

"Hello."

"Hi. It's me, Nayla. Now, you have my personal number in your phone. Lock it in and you can give me a call anytime."

PG responded with a laugh, "Sure will, Ms. Lady. I sure will."

Nayla hung up from PG and immediately called Ming at her office. Angie answered the phone.

"Thank you for calling the Law Offices of La' Ming Foster. This is Angie. How may I help you?"

"Hey, Ang. What's up girl, this is Nayla."

"Nothing much, boo. Working hard or should I say hardly working. What's going on, on your end?"

"Nothing, baby, just trying to make this paper."

"I hear you," Angie said.

"Hey is Ming in?" Nayla asked.

"Yeah, let me put you through to her."

"Okay, baby, talk with you later. Have a good one," Nayla replied.

"You too, baby, talk to you later," Angie said then contacted Ming to transfer the call.

"Hey Ming, Nayla is on line two. Here she is," Angie said as she connected the call.

"Hey girlie girl, what's up, you called me?" Nayla said.

"Yes, yes, yes, girl, what are you doing?"

"I'm driving. I just left from doing an interview."

"Well, you need to pull over for what I'm about to tell you."

"Okay, really? What's up?"

"You know the stud that I have been fantasizing about?"

"Yeah, what about her?"

"Well, I had my meeting with Dominique Carter and her business manager, today. Low and behold, I walk into my conference room and who is sitting there with Dominique, her!!!"

"What?" Nayla asked. "What the hell? Come on. Tell me what else happened."

"Well, I walked in and she was eating. Just as I was getting ready to introduce myself, she looked up and I realized it was her. I almost passed out. I walked in trying to appear calm. I went over to where they were seated. She stood up and shook my hand. I couldn't believe it. I wanted to just say, 'hey, lady you have been on my mind for the last couple of days.'"

"Girl, I know you did. Wow! I can't believe it. So now what?" Nayla asked.

"Well, I tried to get her to let me take her out to dinner for helping me and she said no, but she offered to cook dinner for me this Friday."

"Really, so are you going?" Nayla asked excitedly.

"Of course, she wouldn't take no for an answer. I don't know what to wear or what to do. I am so like a teenager all over again," Ming said smiling the whole time.

"Girl it must be in the air, because I just met a fine assed stud. Remember, I just told you that I was conducting an interview?"

"Yeah," Ming replied.

"Well, I went into this store called Frames to interview the owner. Her name is PG."

"PG? What the hell kind of name is that?"

"Oh, it stands for Parker Glover."

"Oh, I see, continue," Ming said.

"Well, I went into the store early just to take a look around. It had some really great buys. So, as I was looking, a chick came up and was hitting on me. Girl, talking mad shit, you hear me. So, when I went into the dressing room, she told me that she would be waiting for my number when I got out. But, by the time I finished trying on the clothes, she was gone."

"What!" Ming exclaimed. "How many clothes were you trying on?"

"Just a few. Listen, so I went and made my purchases then asked for the owner of the store. Girl, the sales clerk took me into the owner's office. I had a seat and waited for her to come in. Sure as shit the owner was the girl who had been trying to talk to me while I was looking around."

"Girl, you are kidding me."

"No, I'm not. So, she still wanted my number and she wants to take me out to dinner. I don't know, Ming. She's a stud. A fine as fuck stud, but Ming, I just don't know."

"Why Nayla?" asked Ming. "What are you so afraid of? Just let your guard down for once and see where it leads you."

"I know. I guess I should especially since you are getting ready to date a stud. Who knew."

"Who said I was getting ready to date a stud? We are just having dinner."

"Whatever," Nayla laughed. "I never would have thought I would see the day that you would give a stud any kind of chance."

"Well, I never thought I would see the day that you would accept the fact that you are a lesbian, but I guess everything changes with time."

"This is so true, my friend," Nayla said thoughtfully. "Let me get back to driving. I will talk with you later. I love you."

"Okay," Ming replied. "I love you, too."

CHAPTER TEN

Just as Ming was hanging up from Nayla there was a knock on her door.

"Come in," she said.

"Hey," Angie said as she entered Ming's office. "I'm gone for the day. I just wanted to remind you that I was getting off early today."

"Yes," replied Ming. "I didn't forget."

Before Ming could ask her who would be covering for her, Angie said, "I have Michelle covering the front desk in my absence so anything that you will need she can supply. Paula is pulling those documents that you needed scanned."

"Thank you so much."

"I will see you tomorrow, bright and early," Angie said. "I will give you a call later on tonight."

"Okay, hon. Take care and thanks for working everything out before you left," Ming replied.

Whew, so much to do and not enough time. What am I going to do first, Angie thought. As she put her belongings in her car, she decided to drop by and see Rachael before running her errands. But, just as she was getting into the car her phone rang. She looked at the phone and saw that the call was from Tanya. *I know what's up with that*, she thought and let the call go to voicemail. When her phone chimed letting her know a message was received, she picked it up and checked her voicemail.

"Hey you. What's up? I got a taste for some ice cream can you bring it to me?"

Oh, I just may have time to drop that off, Angie thought as she pulled off. Angie wasn't able to go see Rachael at her office due to the call from one of her dips making her do a full detour. Hell, now she wouldn't even get a chance to run her errands.

You see Tanya was an aggressive femme who loved to eat pussy, and she did it very well. From time to time, when she called, it was usually because she wanted a taste and Angie never turned her down.

CHAPTER ELEVEN

Ray walked into Frames a few minutes after Nayla left.

"Hey, man. What's up?" she said as she slapped hands with PG.

"Nothing much, man, just finished my interview for the magazine and, boy, I feel great."

"I'm proud of you," Ray said. "Look at my boi blowing up."

"Yeah, I try. Hey, man. Come with me to run an errand," PG asked.

"Okay, cool."

The two friends walked out of the store, and got into PG's vehicle and drove off.

"Yeah, man. I wanted to say thanks for hooking up those track lights in the store and getting my electro all fixed up."
"No prob, man. That's what friends are for," Ray replied.

" Fo' sho'. You right man so tell me why this fly chick was in the store shopping. You know I was checking her out. Baby girl was fine as hell. So I went over to her and, you know, gave her my charm."

"Yeah, I can image your charm," Ray laughed.

"No, listen, so I'm talking to her and shit, you know, and she picks out a dress to buy. So I said, 'when I take you to dinner I want you to wear that.'"

"Really?" Ray continued laughing. "And what did she say?"

"Man, she started laughing, too, and headed into the dressing room to try on the stuff that she picked out. So I told her I would be waiting for her when she got out of the dressing room, but something came up. I had to go to my office and then to the stock room. But get this, this shit is going to blow your mind. Carla the cashier called me and said someone from the magazine was there waiting for me. So I told her to take them into my office and I would be there shortly. I walk in and, hot damn, it's old girl with the dress that I was trying to holla at."

"Word, dude? You kidding, right?" asked Ray.

"Hell naw, I'm not kidding. So, I tell her, 'hey, look what's up with you and me?'"

"Hey, man, I thought you don't mix business with pleasure?" Ray asked.

"Man, I don't, but girl is fine as hell with hella body. I gots to break that rule. I told her the same thing." They both started laughing.

"So what's up with her?" Ray asked.

"Well, I gave her my cell number. So, when she left the store I watched her get into her car and as soon as she got in she called me and told me to lock in her personal number, which I did. I think I'm gonna call her tonight."

"Man, you crazy," Ray said.

"I know right," PG laughed as the two sped down the street.

~

PG pulled into the parking lot of the radio station.

"Hey, man, we're here. You want to go in or you want to stay out here in the car?" she asked Ray.

"Oh, I think I will just stay in the car. How long are you going to be?"

"It will only take a few minutes. I'll be right back," PG said as she got out of the car then went inside the building.

Just as PG disappeared into the building, Ray realized that she had to use the bathroom. *Damn*, she thought, *I can't hold it. Let me go in here and see if they have a bathroom.*

She exited the car and headed towards the building. As she approached the door, she was surprised to see the DJ that she saw at PG's store. She was walking and texting so she didn't see Ray approach the building.

Ms. Lady, Ray thought as she licked her lips. Instead she said, "Hello there, beautiful," as she held the door open for Kim.

Kim was so busy on her blackberry checking her email that she didn't even see Ray standing there holding the door for her.

She smells divine, Kim thought as she came close to Ray. "Hi, how are you?" she asked.

"I'm good. What about yourself?" Ray responded.

"I'm fine. Just walking and working," laughed Kim.

"Well, you had better be careful. I wouldn't want you to run into something while you're walking and working."

"Well, I'm glad it was you I almost ran into and not the door," said Kim.

"So am I," Ray said as she stood to the side to let Kim enter the building. "After you."

"Hey do you guys have a bathroom in here?"

"Yeah, but it's not a public restroom. Let me scan you in."

"Okay," Ray said as they walked to the restroom area. "I appreciate it."

"No problem. What's your name?" asked Kim as she scanned the door to let her in.

"Raven Jones, but you can call me Ray."

"Pleased to meet you, Ray. I'm Kimberly Brooks. You can call me Kim."

"Okay, Kim, how about I call you later tonight and we talk more?"

"Sure. My cell is 773 589 5452. If I don't answer, text me, and I will certainly call you back."

As Ray was putting Kim's number in her phone she said, "I'm going to call you right now so that you can lock my number in and you will know it's me."

"Oh, yeah," replied Kim, "why, are you looking forward to talking to me?"

"Yes, I am," replied Ray as she called Kim's phone.

"I got it," Kim said.

"Okay, I will let you go ahead and get to work so I can relieve some stress," Ray said as she pointed towards the bathroom.

"I'll talk with you later. Have a good one," Kim said as she walked away.

"You too, baby girl," Ray said as she watched Kim get on the elevator.

Man what were the odds, Ray thought. *I must be one lucky mutha fucka right now. I wanted to meet ole girl and it happened. Wait until I tell PG.* Ray used the bathroom, washed her hands and went back out to the car. *Thank goodness for a full bladder*, she thought as she laughed to herself.

~

Nayla was on her way into Kim's office to connect with her regarding the interview with PG and to establish an interview date with DC. Nayla pulled up in the parking lot and walked passed a car with a stud sitting inside. *Wow*, they are everywhere she thought. *She is fine too.*

"Hello," she said as she walked by the drop top car that the stud was in.

"Hi, how are you, queen?" the stud replied.

Nayla smiled as she went into the building. She walked to the elevator and pushed the button and, as she was waiting for the elevator to come down, she turned to look out of the door to see if she could see the stud in the car. Just then, the elevator came down and the doors opened. She turned around and was face to face with PG.

"Well, hello there, good looking. What a pleasant surprise," PG smiled as she walked off the elevator and got so close to Nayla that she could have kissed her.

"Hello, didn't I just leave you a little while ago? So you do magic tricks, too? Appearing wherever I am?" Nayla asked with a grin.

"Well, I can do any kind of tricks you want, and believe me, they will be magical. Maybe this is a sign that you and I need to start spending time together," PG whispered in Nayla's ear as she walked pass.

"I won't hold you up because I have someone waiting for me, but don't forget about tonight we have a lot to talk about."

"I won't," Nayla said blushing a little bit as she got on the elevator.

PG watched Nayla until the doors closed. *Yeah, I got plans for her*, she thought to herself as she left the building. When PG got to the car, Ray was on the phone so she got in and drove off without speaking.

"Guess what, G?" Ray said as she got off the phone.

"What, man?"

"I ran into the DJ the one that came to your store to tell you about the featured article. Well, technically, she almost ran into me.

"How? Tell me what happened?"

"Well, when you left, I realized I had to use the bathroom. So, I got out the car to go inside to use it and she was walking up the walk way. She was walking and paying attention to her phone so she didn't see me. I said hello. But, long story short, I got her number and I will be calling her later."

"Man, get the fuck out of here. Tell me why I just ran into ole girl? The one I was just telling you about.

"You kidding?"

"Nope, I'm serious as hell."

"Well, you got you one tonight and so do I," Ray laughed as they slapped fives as they drove down the road.

~

Nayla knocked on Kim's office door.

"Come in," she called out.

"Hey, Kim, it's me," Nayla said as she walked into the office.

"Hey, there you. How's it going? What are you all smiles about? Let me in on it, because girl, you cheesing from ear to ear."

"Nothing and no I'm not. I don't know what you are talking about," Nayla said.

"I'm here to tell you that I went to the featured store and met with the owner and got some good information that I needed for the article."

"That's good," Kim said. "I went over my schedule and it seems like I can do the interview with DC in a few weeks, but we will have to move some shows around if she needs it done sooner."

"Ok," Nayla said. "Let me find out for sure before I give the okay. I need to call to see what will fit into DC's schedule."

"Okay, sounds good. I will make some calls, too, to see how soon we can get this done. Hey, why didn't you just give me a call instead of coming all the way down here?" Kim asked.

"I was just in the neighborhood so I thought what the hell, I will stop by."

"Whatever, I know you. You're on PP."

"Don't start Kim." Nayla warned.

"Yes, you are. I see it in your eyes. You are on the pussy prowl. Don't look at me. I'm not giving up any," Kim replied.

"Girl, please, I don't want any, and if I did, I could have it."

"No, you couldn't," Kim said. "You had it once and you won't get it no more."

"Anyway, have a great show. I am out of here."

"See ya," replied Kim.

~

Nayla was pissed because Kim was right. She wanted to have her itch scratched and man she longed for sex with a woman. Kim looked good. She always did, but Nayla knew she fucked that up a long time ago and there would be no going back.

She didn't want to go online and try to find a one night fuck. She didn't want to go to the club to go home with someone to find out their shit ain't right. PG had given her her number and, she had to admit, she was feeling her in every way. Only issue was PG was a stud, but a damn good looking one. *What was she going to do? Damn.*

CHAPTER TWELVE

Ming had finished all of the work she needed to do for the day. She was exhausted, but excited about putting a name to the face she had been thinking about all week. *Damn, what were the odds*, she thought.

As she drove home, Ming fantasized about Kimoni. She even said her name aloud. *What's coming over me? I have never had these strong feelings for a stud, what's up with me?*

When Ming arrived at home, she prepared the bathroom for a long, relaxing bath. She couldn't wait to unwind and give Kimoni a call. She wanted to know what was on her mind. After taking her bath, Ming oiled her body from head to toe with baby oil, sprayed on her night time cologne, and slipped on a silk robe.

Ming retrieved Kimoni's business card from her briefcase. She twirled it around in her hand for a moment. She didn't know what she would say. She picked up her phone and dialed the number.

"Hello," the voice on the other end answered.

"Hi, can I speak to Kimoni?" Ming asked.

"May I ask who's speaking?"

"This is La'Ming Foster."

"Well, hello there, pretty lady," she said. "This is Kimoni. I have been waiting for your call."

"Oh, you have?" asked Ming, a smile creeping across her face.

"Yes, most definitely. How are you this evening?" Kimoni asked.

"I'm great and you?"

"Well, like I said in the meeting today, I am even better now that I found you."

"Really? Why have you been looking for me?"

Kimoni started to chuckle, "You know, I have had you on my mind since that Sunday I fixed your flat."

"Really?" Ming said with a sly smile on her face. "I was so appreciative that you helped me that evening. I wanted to ask your name, but you disappeared so quickly."

"Yeah, I didn't want to, but the roadside assistance guy threw a monkey wrench in the program," Kimoni said. "You looked and smelled so good in your workout clothes."

"Thank you," Ming blushed.

"Who would have thought that the woman whose tire I fixed would have turned out to be DC's potential lawyer."

"Right, it is such a small world," Ming responded as she settled down to chat with Kimoni until the wee hours of the morning.

As PG and Ray were getting out of the car back at PG's store, a group of girls were in the parking lot.

"Hey there, how ya'll doing?" one of the girls called out.

"I'm good, Shorty. What about you?" PG replied as she paused to take a better look at the girls.

"Hey there. What's happening?" Ray waved.

"I'm good," the girl responded. "Well, why don't ya'll come go with us and hang out? Maybe we can get into a little something."

"Yeah, maybe later," PG said.

"Naw, I'll pass," said Ray as she continued into the store.

"So, baby girl, what's your number?" PG asked as she walked to the car where the girls were.

PG came into the store, a few moments later, laughing. Ray was at the counter talking with Carla.

"Hey, man come in my office and let me tell you what just happened," PG said as she walked towards her office. "Hey, man, she wanted me to hook up with her and her friend tonight."

"Word? So, what did you say?"

"I told her to give me her number and I would call her."

Ray laughed as they walked into PG's office. "Well are you? What about the girl you were telling me about from the store earlier?"

"Oh, yeah. I haven't forgotten about baby girl. I am going to call her later on."

"Well, playa playa, I'm outta here. I got something to get into later," Ray announced.

"Yeah, I bet. Just call me later, man," PG said as she stood up to give Ray some dap.

"I will," Ray said as she walked out of PG's office. As Ray walked to her car, she got out her cell phone and called Kim.

"Hi, this is Kim."

"Hey Kim, this is Ray."

"Ray, ummm…"

"Ray. You ran into me at your building today."

"Oh, yes, Ray. How are you? I'm sorry. I was just day dreaming."

"Okay. I hope it was about me," Ray said with a chuckle in her voice. "So what's going on with you?"

"Nothing much. Nothing planned. Why?" Kim asked.

"I was calling to see if you would like to meet up to have a drink right now or maybe some dinner."

"Why, sure," Kim said. "Where would you like to meet?"

"How about Dashes in an hour? I will meet you out front."

"Sure," Kim said. "I will be there."

"Okay, I'll see you then," Ray said then disconnected the call.

Kim was excited to see Ms. Tattoos again. She was already on her way home and didn't have any plans. She was happy that Ray called. She hadn't been out for a while because she was taking a break, as she called it. However, she was ready and willing to get back to dating.

She ran home to freshen up before she met up with Ray. She didn't have time to get redressed so she choose to change her shirt and shoes, put on a little gloss, and fix her hair. She paused to check herself in the mirror before she exited her home to meet Ray.

Kim and Ray pulled up at the same time and parked right next to one another. Ray admired Kim as she got out of her car and walked to the front of Dashes. Ray thought she looked amazing. Ray hurried and jumped out of her car and followed Kim towards the entrance of Dashes.

Ray enjoyed Kim's walk and the way her ass looked in her jeans. She couldn't help imagining what was in them. The words to Ginuwine's song, In Those Jeans, played in her head. She had a big smile on her face when Kim turned around.

"What are you smiling so hard about?" she asked.

"Nothing, baby, just thinking about something."

"Oh, it must be good since you have that big ol' Kool Aid smile on your face," Kim joked.

"Oh, yes it is," Ray grinned. "Shall we?" she asked as she opened the door to the restaurant to allow Kim to enter.

"Table for two," Ray told the hostess.

"This way please," the hostess said as she escorted Ray and Kim to a table.

Ray pulled out the chair for Kim. "Here, my lady, have a seat."

"Why, thank you. Aren't you the perfect gentle stud," Kim replied.

"I try. I do try," Ray said as they both began to look at their menus.

"I'm so hungry," they both said at the same time which caused them to start laughing.

"Get out of my head," Kim chuckled.

"No you get out of mine," Ray laughed.

"Well, I know what I want what about you?" Kim asked Ray.

"Oh, yes, I know what I want, but the question is are you going to give it to me?" Ray said as she took a sip of water and locked eyes with Kim.

"Depends on what it is that you want," Kim replied with a sly grin on her face.

"Oh, really? So how about I tell you in code and then you tell me if I can have what I want."

"Okay. "What kind of codes are we talking?"

Just as Ray was getting ready to explain, the waitress came to the table.

"Sorry to have kept you waiting, my name is Sug and I will be your waitress for tonight. Can I take your order?

"Are you ready to order, Ray," Kim asked.

"Yes, I am, Kim. Go ahead, ladies first."

After they finished with their order, Kim excused herself to go to the ladies' room. She went to the ladies room to wash her hands and make sure her makeup was on point. When Kim got back to the table, her drink was waiting for her.

"Hi, I'm back. Did you miss me?" she said to Ray.

"Yes, you are and I certainly did," Ray responded with a smile. "I've been waiting for you."

"Well, that's good to hear," Kim said as she sat down and took a sip of her drink. "So, tell me a little about yourself."

Ray began to tell Kim a little about herself, what she did for a living, etcetera. They both talked about everything under the sun including what they were looking for in a mate. It felt like they knew each other previously. Neither Kim nor Ray wanted the night to end. They were really enjoying each other's company.

Kim picked up her drink and said, "Let's toast."

"To what?" Ray asked.

"To new beginnings," she said.

Ray picked up her glass and said, "To new beginnings."

They both took a sip of their drinks. They were both thinking about the same thing as they looked at each other and made their toast, but neither one

157

wanted to say it out loud. Both of them had thoughts of being intimate.

"Dinner was great," Kim said. "Thank you so much for asking me out."

"Thank you for being beautiful. I am really enjoying your company. How about you come back to my place and we continue on with this night?" Ray asked Kim while caressing her fingers.

"I would love to," Kim said while thinking, *oh boy would I love too.* "However, I can't. I have something to do early tomorrow. Can I take a rain check on that? Maybe this weekend coming up?" she asked Ray with a sexy smile on her face. "I promise I will make it up to you."

Ray licked her lips, "Sure, we can get into something else this weekend. I look forward to you making it up to me. Why don't you tell me how you plan on doing it?" Ray said with a devilish grin?

"Oh, stop. You are just going to have to wait and see," Kim replied as she finished the last of her drink.

"Okay, cool," Ray said as she motioned for the waitress so she could pay the bill.

As the two walked out of the restaurant, Ray held the door open for Kim. She grabbed Kim by the hand and walked her to her car.

"Hey, let me have your keys," Ray said as she took the keys from Kim and unlocked her door.

"My, my, you are the perfect gentle stud," Kim exclaimed.

"I try to be," Ray smiled and leaned forward to kiss Kim on the lips.

Kim closed her eyes and slowly let down her guard as Ray pulled her closer into her arms and gently inserted her tongue into Kim's mouth. Their tongues danced around like synchronized swimmers. They both wanted more than just this kiss, but now wasn't the time.

CHAPTER THIRTEEN

Kim woke up thinking about the kiss that she and Ray shared in the parking lot after they finished dinner. Ray's lips were so soft and her tongue exploded with great flavor. *I can only image what would have happen if I went home with her*, she thought. The music from her phone vibrating made her jump. *Damn, work is always calling*, but, to her surprise, it was a text message from Ray.

I enjoyed last night looking forward to seeing you again have a great day Ray!

Kim replied expressing her satisfaction with the evening and her desire to get together again real soon.

It had been awhile since she had given any thought to dating someone on a serious note. For all of the ladies she came across, it was strictly for her to have fun with. She didn't have time for the drama that came alone with being in a steady relationship. Although, being single came with drama too.

Kim got up and went to the shower to get ready for work. It was almost 12 o'clock. *Time is money and I got to get mine*, she thought.

~

Ray was picking up some supplies when she texted Kim and, to her surprise, Kim texted right back. *Oh, good, she wants to hook up again. Cool maybe sometime this weekend*, she thought as she texted Kim back.

Hey you. Sounds good. How about we play it by ear and maybe we can do something late Saturday or early Sunday?

Ray hit the send button and awaited Kim's response. She was really feeling her and wanted to get to know her a lot better.

When Kim got out of the shower, she saw that she had another text from Ray. She responded immediately.

Let me see how my schedule is looking for those days and I will let you know.

She hit the send button on her phone.

Okay, cool, baby girl, sounds good. Now you have a wonderful day. Talk with you soon.

Ray hit the send button on her phone.

As Kim was drying off and oiling her body, the text from Ray came through. Kim read the text and thought, *yeah, I would really like to get to know this stud.*

161

She has this vibe about her. I can't call it, but damn I want it.
Kim texted Ray back to have a great day and with
smooches attached to conclude the text conversation.

Kim laughed to herself as she hit the music on
her entertainment center. House music poured out of
her speaker system. "Oh that's my shit," she said as
the song It's Time For The Perculator. She began
dancing around her bedroom. *This is a workout by its*
self, she thought. *Who needs the gym when you got house*
music? Oh, damn, let me get my ass ready and get out the door.
I can't be jerking my body right now. I have to make it to
work for the doughnuts, she thought as she turned off the
CD playing and left for work.

Ming instructed Angie to have some documents sent to Rachael at her job. Angie decided she would take them down herself at the end of the day that way she could visit her friend and shoot the shit. When Angie arrived, there was a lot going on in the hotel lobby. She walked up to the front desk.

"Hello," said the clerk. "How may I help you?"

"Hi, how are you doing?" Angie responded. "Is Ms. Wilson in?"

"Why, yes. She's right around the corner in Conference Room B. Just one moment while I page her for you."

"No, that won't be necessary I will just walk over there. Just as Angie was about to turn the corner, the sexy caterer, who brought the sandwiches to the office early that week, walked up.

"Good evening, Ms. Hill. How are you doing?" Angie asked as the two stood face to face.

"Well hello, Ms. Angie. I'm fine just a little busy right now. I have to set up the food and beverages for a photo shoot this evening. How are you?"

"I'm good. I don't mean to hold you up. Have a good rest of your day," Angie said as she walked away. "Oh, and by the way, your food was delicious. I can't wait to try something else."

"Thanks for the compliment and you have a good day as well," Stony replied and hurried away.

Angie walked into the conference room where Rachel was located. It had been transformed into a tropical paradise.

"Hey there you," she said to Rachael.

"Hey boo. What's up?" Rachael asked.

"I have the documents that Ming wanted me to send over, but I just decided to bring them to you."

"Okay, thank you, I was waiting on these."

"You're welcome," Angie replied. "Wow it looks great in here. What's going on?"

"A photographer booked the conference room to do a photo shoot this evening. I'm just making sure everything is where and how it is supposed to be. What's going on for tonight?" she asked Angie.

"Nothing much. What about you? Got any plans?"

"Nope, just working late, right now. I'm going to wait until the client arrives to make sure everything is good, then I'm going to leave. You want to wait for me?"

"Sure, why not?" Angie said as she picked up a strawberry and bit into it.

"Plus, I see something else on the menu I want to taste!" she smirked.

"I just bet you do," Rachel laughed. "Let me finish up here. Go ahead and take a bite out of your forbidden fruit."

"Oh, I plan on it," Angie replied.

As she walked out of the room, Angie thought about how she was going to strike up another conversation with Stony. As she made her way to Rachael's office, she ran into Stony again.

"Hey there you," she said. "I just had a taste of your fruit and I must say it was delish."

Smiling, Stony shook her head and said, "Thanks, I'm glad you liked the fruit."

"Oh, I did, and I would like a little more. You wanna give me some?"

"Girl, you are too much I need to finish setting up," Stony laughed as she held up a container.

"Okay, I don't want to disturb your perfection of work. I will just have to call and order some more of your sandwiches for work."

"Yes, you do that," Stony replied as she walked away.

Man, she is playing hard to get, Angie thought. But what Angie wants Angie gets, and you, I will have, Angie said to herself as she watched Stony walk away.

Angie continued to Rachael's office to wait for her, all the while, thinking of how she could get a piece of Stony's fine self.

~

As Stony finished setting up the food for the shoot, she thought about Angie and her persistence. *What were the odds of continuing to run into her?* Stony wondered if she would make good on her promise to order some more food.

While Stony continued to muse, she cleaned up the remaining odds and ends for the buffet. Shortly after, the photographer entered the room and introduced herself.

"Hi, I'm Dee. I'm the photographer for the shoot."

"Hi, I'm the caterer. I just finished setting up for your shoot," Stony replied as she extended her hand in greeting. "Everything is laid out against the wall, as requested."

"Yes, it looks very good," she replied and walked away to begin setting up as Stony packed up her containers.

Done packing up, Stony said good-bye to the photographer and walked out of the door. She ran into Rachael who was coming in the door.

"Hi, Ms. Wilson, I am done setting up the food for the shoot. You have a good evening."

"You too," Rachael replied as she continued into the conference room.

The photographer was setting up her equipment when Rachael walked in.

"Good evening. I'm Ms. Wilson, the hotel's manager," Rachael announced as she extended her hand.

The photographer replied, "Hi, I'm Dee."

"Please, if there is anything that you need, just let me or one my staff members know. We are here to accommodate you in every way."

"Thanks," replied Dee, "if I need anything, I will certainly let you know."

"Well, it looks as if you have everything under control. I will be in my office. Take care. Have a great shoot."

"Sounds good. Thanks, and if I need anything, I know where to find you," Dee replied not looking up from her photography bag.

Rachael left the conference room and headed straight to her office to go over the documents that Ming sent. Angie was deep in thought about Stony when Rachael walked into her office.

"Hey, girl. I am going to be here for a while. I'm going to have to take a rain check."

"Okay," Angie said. "Call me later, if it doesn't get too late. "No, scratch that, let me call you tomorrow. I may get into something tonight, or better yet, someone may be getting into me."

"I do not want to know about it," Rachael said laughing. "I love you, but I don't want to hear about your adventures."

"Yes, you do, because your sex life is sooo boring. All of your adventure is through me."

"Whatever, I have to get back to work please," Rachel laughed.

"Okay, I'm going. I have something I need to work on, too. Bye, boo," Angie said as she left Rachael's office.

While she looked through the documents, Rachael thought about DC, how she was a potential RL, and how she really wanted to see her again to put on her charm. If given the chance, she would get DC and make DC hers. What Rachael wants, Rachael gets, no matter who it is and DC is what she wanted. Rachael was on a mission to get it.

DC was very attractive and so was her money. She had everything that Rachael wanted and needed to live a lavish life. The money and the fame could take her to new heights. Maybe her ship had come in and she would hit the jackpot with DC.

She didn't care that people thought she was a gold digger. She did what she had to do to get the finer things in life. It's not that she couldn't get them on her own, but why should she? *What's wrong with getting things for her time? Hell I'm a beautiful woman who needs to be compensated*, she thought. *Nothing in life is free and certainly not my time.*

Now she only needed to find a way to see her again. She knew Ming wasn't going to help her with this. So she would have to do a little research to find out a little more about DC. Rachel continued to muse and plot on DC's take down.

CHAPTER FOURTEEN

DC had a photo shoot she had to do this evening. She didn't have to prepare much. Everything would be provided once she got to the hotel. DC wished the shoot would have been a little earlier so she could have enjoyed the beautiful night weather. But, this was the nature of the business and she had to roll with the money. DC called Kimoni to let her know that she was on her way to the gig.

"Hey, what's up?" Kimoni said when she answered the phone.

"Hey, man, I'm on my way to the photo shoot."

"Okay, cool. Call me once you're done. I'm getting ready for my evening tonight."

"Okay, man, will do. Peace." DC replied and she hung up the phone.

While driving to the hotel, DC thought about her life and how blessed she was and no matter what she wasn't going to let neither money nor fame change her.

DC arrived and entered the hotel lobby. She approached the front desk and addressed the clerk sitting there.

"Hi, I'm here for the photo shoot."

"Yes, right this way to the conference room," the clerk said as she came from around the counter. The clerk escorted DC to the conference room.

"Wow, the room looks gorgeous," the clerk gushed as she entered the conference room.

"Why, thank you, baby," said one of the prop directors. "We try to make it look like the real thing."

The conference room had been transformed into a beautiful tropical getaway.

"Well, you have certainly done that," DC said. "Where do I get ready?"

"Right over here," the photographer chimed in. "Hi, I'm Dee. I will be shooting you today."

"Nice to meet you," DC replied. "Just tell me what to do."

"Well, go right through there and change and I will be waiting for you here."

DC went to change into the first outfit for the shoot.

~

"Yes! You look great," Dee said to DC. "Come and stand right here," she said pointing. "Now give me attitude." Dee took picture after picture.

The camera lights and the camera action was all DC thought about as the shoot began. She posed and smiled and was really having a great time with this shoot.

"Now take your glasses and tip them down. Yea, like that. That's great. Now turn to the side. Oh, just like that. I am feeling this. Now lift up your shirt like this and let me see them stomach muscles."

Just as DC was lifting up her shirt and doing poses, Rachael walked in to check to see how the shoot was going. Rachael looked around in awe of what was once her conference room that was now a tropical getaway.

Oh my goodness, she thought, *I didn't know that DC was the client that was doing the shoot today.* Rachael looked up to the sky and mouthed the words, thank you. *Fuck, DC was sexy as hell. Oh, I wonder what it would be like to have her between my legs*, she thought as she sucked in her bottom lip. With every click of the camera, Rachael saw DC in a different light. *Umm... I want that for myself.*

DC was really enjoying this photo shoot. The photographer, Dee, was cooler than a muther and that made working with her easier. Out of the corner of her eye, she could see that someone was watching her and to her surprise, that someone was Ms. Wilson. *Rachael*, she thought to herself. *I wonder what she is doing here and how did she know I was here. She certainly looked good.*

"Hey, I need for you to kneel down and turn to the side. Let me see those lips. Yes, yes that's it. Ok tilt your head and look up for me. Perfect, perfect. You are a dream to work with. Okay, everyone take five. I need to reload," shouted Dee.

Perfect, DC thought, *that will give me some time to talk to Rachael and see what's up with her.* DC walked over to the buffet table and grabbed a bottle of water. She walked over to where Rachael was standing and hi to her.

"Hello, Ms. Wilson isn't it?"

"Yes," said Rachael as she extended her hand, "but you can call me Rachael."

"Hi, Rachael, fancy meeting you here. How are you?"

"I'm fine," Rachael said. "How about you?"

"I'm good, just working."

"So am I," Rachael replied.

"Really?" DC responded looking kind of surprised.

"Yeah, I manage the hotel here."

"Wow, small world," DC replied.

"Yeah, it is. Who would have ever thought I would host a photo shoot for the famous Dominique Carter," Rachael said with a smile.

"Of all the hotels that could have been chosen, I'm glad it was this one that was picked to have this shoot," DC said. "So, tell me, how do you like the view of the photo shoot so far?"

"Oh, well the scenery is great and I like what I see."

"Do you now? Well, how about once I'm done, if it's not too late, we go out and get to know each other a little better."

"Really? I think I could arrange for that to happen."

"Well, I hope you can. Let's work out the details once I'm done," DC said as she took a sip of her water.

"Okay people, let's rock and roll," Dee commanded as she picked up her camera.

"That's my cue," DC said as she winked at Rachael and walked away. "Hey," she said as she turned back around to face Rachael. "Stick around and watch the shoot. You will no doubt like what you see."

"Okay, I think I will do that, but first I must make my rounds."

"I'll be looking for you," DC replied as she stepped up to the prop to begin shooting again.

Wow what are the odds to have DC here at my job? No need to go looking for anything. She came to me instead, Rachael thought as she walked to the front desk to check on her staff and to ensure everything was okay for the night shift.

After making her rounds, Rachael went to her office to freshen up a bit. She always kept toothpaste and a toothbrush in her desk. She wanted to have extra fresh breath just in case she and DC shared a kiss. She took one final look in her mirror. *Perfect,* she thought as she walked out of the door, locked her office door and headed to the conference room to charm the fuck out of her new RL.

Rachael entered the tropical getaway for a second time. DC looked spectacular. Her abs were like, damn. She had on a sports bra with her jeans pulled down showing the sides of a strap. Man, looking at DC like that made Rachael want to take her home and fuck the shit out of her. Although that would be breaking her rule of 'before any ass is passed she must get some cash.' *It just might be more than just money with this one*, she mused looking at DC with pure lust in her eyes. The shouting of Dee bringing the shoot to an end snapped Rachael out of her trance.

DC and Dee were talking when Rachael walked up to them.

"Hi ladies."

"Hello, Ms. Wilson," both DC and Dee said at the same time.

"Wow, you guys were great," Rachael said.

"Thank you," they both answered.

"Well, it's been a great pleasure working with you, DC. You are an easy client."

"Thanks, Dee," DC responded as she shook her hand. "You were a great photographer."

Dee walked over to the buffet table and began fixing herself something to eat.

"Well, Miss Lady, how did you like watching me work?"

"Oh you looked great, I must say," Rachael replied. "It was my first time on a photo shoot."

"I'm glad you liked what you saw. So let me ask you, are you hungry?"

Looking at her watch Rachael replied, "Yes, I am, but it's kind of late. I really don't want anything too heavy."

"Okay, well, how about this? You come home with me and let me cook you a late night, light dinner," DC said.

"Home with you? How do I know you won't bite?" Rachael replied.

"I'm a gentleman and I will only bite if you want me too," DC said laughing.

"Funny. I like a sense of humor but how about we make it for tomorrow. Can we go for lunch or maybe an early dinner?" Rachael asked.

"I will have to check my schedule. How about we exchange numbers and I give you a call."

"Sounds good to me," Rachel said and she gave DC her number.

"Okay, Ms. Rachael, until tomorrow. Have a good rest of the night," DC said as she left and went to her car.

Rachael couldn't believe it. She had DC's number and they were going to have a lunch date tomorrow. Her plan was working out better than she thought.

Once DC got to her car, she called Kimoni to give her an update, but only reached her voicemail. DC hung up deciding that she would rather talk than leave a message. She disconnected the line and drove home.

CHAPTER FIFTEEN

Nayla had just come back from getting Chinese food from the restaurant around the corner from her house. She could never get enough of Chinese food. She walked into the kitchen and sat the food down on the counter then went over to the sink to wash her hands. She pulled down a plate and began to fix her dinner for the night. Then, she popped her plate into the microwave to ensure her food was piping hot. She hated room temperature food.

While her food was heating up, Nayla took off her shoes and headed to the bath room to wash her face. When her food was ready, she retrieved her plate from the microwave and sat down at the kitchen counter on one of the stools.

She went over the day's events as she ate her dinner. She played back the scene with PG over and over in her mind. *What should I do*, she thought? *This is crazy. Here I am longing for a woman's touch and I have a woman that seems to be longing to touch me.* "Nuts!!" she said out loud.

Nayla finished her food, put her plate in the sink, and went straight for the bathtub. *A long hot bubble bath will help me work this out*, she thought. Nayla ran the water and added some of her relaxing bath beads to luxuriate the experience.

As she undressed and put her hair up, she thought about how nice it would be to have someone there taking a bath with her. That someone being PG. Nayla slipped into the hot bath, turned on the whirlpool jets and closed her eyes. The warmth of the water along with the sound of the jets started to relax her a bit. Just as she was about to drift off she heard her phone ring.

Damn, she thought. *I'm not getting out of this tub*, but then she remembered it might be PG calling. So she got out of the tub to answer her phone, but by the time she got to it, it had stopped ringing. She was right. It was PG. She hit the call back button as she walked back to get in the tub. Just as she sat back down in the water, PG answered.

"Well, hello there, Ms. Lady. How are you doing?" she asked Nayla.

"I'm good," Nayla said. "How are you?"

"I'm good and will be even better when we go out. So, what are you doing?"

"I'm in the tub."

"Oh, baby girl, really? Don't tell me that. Now you have me thinking about your naked body and what I would love to do to it."

"Oh, really?" Nayla replied.

"Yes. You are very beautiful with a body to match. And, now you calling me while you're all in the nude? Damn, talk about teasing me."

"I'm so sorry is there anything I can do to make it up to you?" Nayla asked.

"Yeah, it is, but only if you're down."

"What is it?"

"Well, since I can't be there with you… Masturbate for me," PG said.

"Excuse me?" Nayla said.

"Come on, baby. You know you want to. I can tell that pussy ain't been tapped in a while. So, let me hear you pleasure yourself. I can't get to you and you're already ready to do it… So, come on," PG pleaded.

"Why should I masturbate for you? I don't even know you."

"Right," PG said. "This is our first step in having safe sex. Now, put me on speaker phone."

Nayla did as PG commanded by putting her on speaker.

"Come on, baby, take the fingers on your left hand and put them in your mouth then touch your lips. Get your fingers wet. Suck on them. Now, baby, put your right hand in your bath water and get it wet. Take your right hand and run it down to your chest. Squeeze your breast ever so softly. Is your head back?" PG asked.

"No."

"Lay your head back as you caress both of your breasts. Think of your hands as my hands."

"Ooh..." Nayla moaned as she twirled her nipples in her fingers.

"Now, baby, have you gotten your nipples hard for me?" PG asked.

"Yes," answered Nayla.

"Now take your bath towel and squeeze some water over your chest and down to your stomach. Take your right hand and rub from the top to the bottom of your pussy for me. Slowly now. Don't rush. Rub your breasts as you rub the top of your pussy."

"Omm…," Nayla moans.

"You like that don't you, baby? So, why don't you take your first two fingers and slowly rub your pussy lips on the outside then the inside."

"Umm… umm…," Nayla moans.

"Don't you touch that clit, yet. Keep rubbing those lips for me baby. Now take your left hand and grab your right breast. Take your tongue and make circles around your nipples for me baby. Nice and slow. Put your nipple in your mouth and flick it around with your tongue. Now take your index finger and rub that clit for me. Wet isn't she?"

"Umm… hun. It feels so good," Nayla replied.

"I know. I know. Now rub that clit up and down. I want you to make it hard and swollen for me. Play with that clit like it was your only toy."

Nayla threw her head back and closed her eyes. She imagined that it was PG's tongue caressing her clit and not her own hand. With each stroke of her finger it felt like PG's wet tongue was sending her to pleasure. Her body jerked intensely in response to the wonderful feeling. She had masturbated before, but never like this.

"How does it feel? Tell me how it feels."

"Good. So good," replied Nayla.

"Now, I want you to stand up and sit on the edge of the tub. I want your feet to be still in the water."

"Okay," Nayla said. "Why?"

"Sshhhh... Don't ask any questions. Now sit on the edge of your tub with your legs spread wide. Imagine me on my knees with my head between your thighs."

"Ohh," Nayla let out a moan that made PG quiver.

"Now, I want you to rub that clit and then take your finger down to your hole."

"Okay," said Nayla.

"Stick it in a little bit and slowly take it out. Now rub your clit. That's my tongue playing with it making it hard. Now slide your finger back to your hole and put them inside one by one. Slowly, in and out, getting all that juice. Now, take them out and put them in your mouth. Lick your juice from your fingers, baby. That's enough licking. Now, put your first two fingers inside your hole. It's dripping wet ain't it, baby?"

"Yes, yes," Nayla exclaimed.

"Now I want you to finger fuck yourself and make that pussy cum for me."

Nayla did as she was told and finger fucked herself in and out. She guided her finger in her pussy. Wetter and wetter, her love hole became as she inserted her fingers one by one. The moment became like a scene from a movie. Nayla fucked herself with passion and force. With every touch of her own hand, she imagined it was PG's strap. Oh, how she wanted it to be PG fucking her instead of her own hand.

"Ooh ooh," is all she could utter as PG guided her.

"Cum," PG said through the phone.

Now was the time she was going to explode and explode she did. "Oh! Oh! Oh! Oh! Oh!" Nayla cried.

"Tell me, baby, is it coming?"

"Yes!" Nayla screamed and creamed all over the side of her tub. She had never experienced anything like that before. "Oh! Oh!" is all PG heard her scream.

Nayla picked up the phone and took it off of speaker.

"You okay, baby?" PG asked.

An out of breath Nayla could barely get her words together. "Yes, oh yes. I'm fine. Damn. Ummm… that was good and it felt good.

"Baby, did it help to have me walk you through masturbating?" PG asked.

"Yes, it did," replied Nayla. "I can't believe I just did that with you on the phone."

"Well, believe it," PG said. "It's just the beginning. Thank you for allowing me to hear you pleasure yourself. It was great. I have a lot of plans for us."

Nayla had got back into her bath water. She tried to compose herself. "Plans? What kind of plans?" she asked in a weak tired voice.

"Oh, you will have to wait and see," PG replied. "I know you are tired so muah," PG gave Nayla a kiss through the phone. "I'm going to let you get some rest. You won't be any good tomorrow if you don't."

"Good night," Nayla said. "I will call you tomorrow afternoon."

"Yes, it was," said PG. "I'll talk to you tomorrow. Sweet dreams." PG hung up the phone.

Nayla sat in the tub for a moment trying to absorb what just happened. She was in disbelief, but felt good all over. *What have I gotten myself into*, she thought as she began to wash up.

CHAPTER SIXTEEN

The next day Ming found herself a little tired from all of the work she had been doing to land DC as a client. *I am going to take the day off and pamper myself and now I can get that briefcase I have been wanting*, she thought. She would call the office later, since it was early, and let Angie know she wouldn't be coming in today. *What the hell, I'll just leave her a voicemail.*

"Hey, Angie, it's me, Ming. I won't be in today, but I am going to need for you to..." Ming finished leaving Angie a message with instructions for the day then disconnected the phone.

Heck, it's Friday, I can play hooky. She would be having dinner with Kimoni so she didn't want to be over worked for their first date. Ming climbed back into bed and turned on her iPod. The smooth voice of Lathun began to play.

Umm, yes the perfect song for how I am feeling. Fortunate. With that thought, Ming drifted back to sleep.

~

Since it was her off day, Nayla slept late. Her body was still trying to recover from last night. When she finally did get up, the clock on the side of her bed read 12:45 p.m.

She stretched and yawned hard. *Oh wee*, she thought, *I am out of it*. "Come on get yourself together," she said to herself. She reached over and grabbed her cell phone. She just had to call Ming to tell her what the hell happened last night. She dialed Ming's office and Angie answered the phone.

"Thank you for calling the law office of La'Ming Foster. This is Angie speaking. How may I help you?"

"Hey, Angie, it's me, Nayla. What's up, boo."

"Nothing much," Angie said. "Trying to get all this work done that Miss Ming has me doing."

"I hear you. Is she in her office?" Nayla asked.

"Nope. She didn't come in today. She may be at home or shopping who knows with Ming." They both started laughing.

"I know, right. She always got some shit going on," Nayla replied.

"You got it," Angie said. "Hey, I got to go. I have another call on the line. Talk with you later, boo. Love ya."

"Love you, too," Nayla said as they hung up the phone.

Nayla called Ming on her cell phone just in case she was out shopping. The ringing of her cell phone is what woke Ming up.

"Hello," she said in a sleepy voice.

"Hey girl, get up," Nayla said. "You still sleeping?"

"What time is it?" Ming asked.

"Girl, it's almost 1 o'clock. Rise and shine. Time to face the world, plus I have something I need to tell you ASAP!"

"What, what is it?" Ming asked.

Just as she was getting ready to start, Ming got a call on her other line. She looked at the caller ID it was Kimoni.

"Hold on, Nayla. I have another call coming in." "Hello," Ming said.

"Hello, sexy," Kimoni said. "How are you this afternoon?"

"I'm fine."

"Yes, you are," Kimoni replied. "Well, I was just calling to hear your voice."

"Why, that's so sweet, but can I call you back?" she asked.

"No need, darling. I'll just see you tonight at 8."

"Okay," replied Ming. "I will see you then." She hung up the phone with Kimoni with such a warm feeling inside.

Ming clicked back over to Nayla. "What's up, love," she said, "is something wrong?"

"No, nothing like that. It's just, remember I told you yesterday about PG?"

"P who?" asked Ming in a surprised voice.

"PG, the stud from the store, the owner!"

"Yeah, yeah, go on."

"Well, I called her last night. Actually, she called me first and I missed the call because I was in the tub. I got out because I wanted to see if it her that was her calling, and it was. So, I called her back. Girl, what I do that for, because man oh man."

"Oh what? Tell me what happened, girl. Spill it!"

"Well, we didn't really do nothing."

"You what? Tell me, tell me!"

"I told her I was in the tub soaking, just unwinding. From there she told me how beautiful I was and how I was teasing her since I called her while, I was in the tub. So I asked her was there anything I could do and she said yes."

"Okay, okay, continue," Ming said.

"Well, she asked me to masturbate for her."

"WHAT!!! Are you serious girl? What! Did you do it? You did it didn't you? OMG, no you didn't! Please finish telling me this."

"Girl, yes, I did do it and, I must say, it was off the chain! I couldn't believe that I actual did that! I did it while she told me what to do and she listened to me moan. Oh girl, I'm telling you that it was some freaky shit."

"What is her sign?" Ming asked laughing.

"Girl, I don't know," Nayla replied. "I will have to get that on our next session." Nayla continued to tell Ming about the events from the night before. She didn't know what she was going to do, but one thing she did know; after last night, she didn't trust herself with PG.

Ming didn't quite know what to think about what Nayla had just told her, but hell, it sounded like she really enjoyed it and she needed something or someone to get her out of her shell. Ming couldn't stop thinking about Kimoni and how she seemed so intriguing and so damned good looking. She wanted to make a good impression on her and she just couldn't wait until their date tonight.

Ming didn't understand this new found attraction she had towards Kimoni. Kimoni was everything Ming avoided. She didn't date studs, period. She just wasn't interested. But, she just didn't know what it was about Kimoni that piqued her interest.

Ming got up and started to get ready for her date. She had a new found excitement like she was back in college and just starting out.

CHAPTER SEVENTEEN

Kimoni didn't want anything to go wrong. Just as she was putting the finishing touches on the table, her phone rang.

"Hello?" she answered. It was Tony, the doorman.

"Ms. Grey, you have a guest."

"Oh, please send her up. Thank you, Tony."

"You're welcome, Ms. Grey. Have a good night."

"You do the same," she said as she hung up the phone.

Eight o'clock sharp, she thought. Ming was right on time and Kimoni couldn't be happier.

"Come on in, beautiful," she said to Ming when she opened the door.

"Thank you," replied Ming. "You're looking good yourself."

"I try," said Kimoni.

"What a lovely place you have here," Ming said as she walked into the beautifully set up condo.

"Thanks again. I did all of the decorating myself."

"Well, you have exquisite taste," Ming said.

"In more ways than one," Kimoni said in a devilish way.

Ming smiled and said, "Point taken."

"Your smile is so beautiful," Kimoni said admired Ming.

"Come on in the dining room. Are you ready to have dinner?"

"Yes," said Ming.

"Well, I have prepared a wonderful meal for a wonderful woman." Ming followed Kimoni into her dining room.

"Wow, the table decor is impressive and dinner smells great. What are you preparing?" Ming asked.

"Just a little bit of this and that," replied Kimoni as she pulled out the chair for Ming to have a seat. "You don't mind if I put on some music, do you?"

"No, not at all," Ming replied.

Kimoni went to her CD player and popped in a CD.

"What kind of wine would you like, red or white?"

"Red, please."

Kimoni disappeared into the kitchen and returned with a bottle of red wine. Kimoni poured them both a glass then left to prepare the plates for them to dine.

~

"Dinner was delicious. Thank you for cooking for me."

"It was my pleasure. Are you done? Would you like any more or some dessert?"

"Oh no, I couldn't eat another bite," Ming followed Kimoni into the room were the music was playing.

"Here, have a seat. Make yourself comfortable."

Kimoni and Ming sat down and began chatting.

"You know I have had you on my mind since that Sunday I fixed your flat."

"Really?" Ming said with a sly smile on her face. "You were looking really good, too, and I was so appreciative that you helped me that evening. I wanted to ask your name but you disappeared so quickly."

"I am so glad that a chance of fate brought us back together."

"Really?" Ming said. "I must admit that I had been thinking of you, also. I usually don't date studs and you had me intrigued for a while.

"Really?" Kimoni said as she moved closer to Ming.

Kimoni leaned in and kissed Ming on her lips. *Her lips were soft as silk and she tastes so divine,* Kimoni thought. Ming took Kimoni in, she smelled intoxicating. This kiss was something she had been waiting for all night.

They kissed and kissed and it was leading to something else, just as they were going to take it a step further there was a knock at the door.

"Are you expecting someone?" Ming asked.

"No. I'm not sure who that could be. Just one moment."

Kimoni went to the door to see who had interrupted her special moment with Ming. As Kimoni looked through her peephole, she couldn't see the face of the person knocking on the door.

"Who is it?" Kimoni exclaimed.

"It's Ms. Jackson from across the hall," the voice replied.

Kimoni turned to Ming, "Oh, it's my neighbor," she said as she opened the door.

Ms. Jackson said, "I am so sorry to bother you this late, Kimoni, but I need some help over in my unit. Would you mind coming over?"

"Sure," said Kimoni. "I will be right there."

Ms. Jackson was an older lady who lived across the hall. She was up there in age and from time to time whenever she needed help Kimoni would assist her. But, damn, thought Kimoni, tonight of all nights.

"I will be right back," Kimoni said in a disappointed voice to Ming.

Ming thought it was so cute and very admirable the way Kimoni helped no matter who it was. It was just as well. They had just met, and if they had not been interrupted, they would have taken it to the next level. Ming wouldn't have minded seeing that she hasn't had any in a while, but she also didn't want to seem easy. She closed her eyes to listen to the music that was playing in the background.

Enchanted by the music Ming didn't notice Kimoni's returned, she opened her eyes to Kimoni standing in front of her singing.

"Come on, baby, take my hand. Let's dance." Kimoni said softly.

"You have a lovely voice," Ming said.

"Why, thank you," Kimoni responded as she finished singing.

Ming leaned her head on Kimoni's shoulder as she sang and they danced until the song was complete.

"Wow, thank you. No one has ever sang to me. That was wonderful."

"Well, you are a wonderful woman," Kimoni said as she pulled Ming closer. Ming looked into Kimoni's eyes. She saw something that she never had before and that was comfort. They shared a kiss that seemed like it shook the room. They continued to kiss and kiss until it seemed as if it would never end.

~

Kimoni led Ming to her bedroom. She wanted to taste her so badly. The hardness in her clit and the pounding of her heart made her feel more anxious.

Ming was wet beyond belief. She was feeling things she had never felt before. Kimoni brought out a rising in her that she had never known. *How could this be?* She wanted her to be between her legs. For her tongue to lick ever spot on her body. She was burning with fire to have Kimoni inside of her, to take her however she wanted.

Kimoni kissed Ming from the top of her neck down to her shoulders. Ming let out a purr that made Kimoni's nature rise even more. Kimoni unbuttoned Ming's shirt to show her sexy bra covering perfect breasts.

Ming caressed Kimoni's hair as Kimoni whispered in Ming's ear, "You're so fucking sexy, baby."

Kimoni twirled her tongue in Ming's ear making her moan. Kimoni removed Ming's shirt and slowly licked down the middle of her chest as she unclasped Ming's bra.

Ming threw her head back in ecstasy.

Taking Ming's breasts in her hands, Kimoni circled Ming's nipples, flicking them with her tongue, teasing her. She took turns on each breast, giving them both the same amount of attention.

Kimoni knelt down and put her hand under Ming's skirt, caressing her thighs. She made her way to Ming's dripping, wet, love hole and she slowly rubbed her pussy with her panties still on. The wetness had soaked through Ming's lace, thong panties.

Kimoni looked up and asked, "Is all that for me?"

"Yes," Ming responded.
With Ming's wetness still on her hand Kimoni pulled her hand from under Ming's skirt and put her

fingers in her mouth. She began caressing Ming's wet pussy, again, through her panties.

Man her pussy smells so fucking good and tastes even better, Kimoni thought.

She looked up at Ming and said, "Are you ready for me to make love to you? Is this what you want?"

Ming leaned over and took Kimoni's face into her hands as she looked into her eyes and began to kiss her and say yes. While still kissing, Ming began to take off Kimoni's shirt.

Kimoni laid Ming on the bed. She began to stroke her pussy with one hand while caressing her breasts with the other.

Oh, it feels so good, thought Ming, damn.

Kimoni begin to lick Ming from the top of her lips down to her breasts, each nipple, the middle of her chest then down to her belly button. While licking and kissing her stomach, Kimoni unbuttoned Ming's skirt.

"Stand up, baby," she said to Ming.

As Ming stood up, her skirt hit the floor revealing her fully exposed breasts, thong and garter stockings. Kimoni was in heaven. *Damn*, she thought. She got closer to Ming and got on her knees. The smell of Ming's sweet pussy had her in a trance. She begins to kiss Ming up her thighs.

With every kiss, Ming got wetter and wetter. She thought she was going to explode. Kimoni undid the straps on Ming's stockings. She rolled her stockings down one by one to reveal her beautiful, brown skin. As Ming stepped out of her stockings, Kimoni kissed her feet. Once the stocking were off, the only thing left was Ming's thong. Still on her knees, Kimoni got closer to Ming's love hole.

"Mmm…," she murmured as she took in her scent. Kimoni knew that she was going to make love to Ming like she had never had it done before.

~

Kimoni was awakened by Ming gently planting kisses on her lips. They shared a very passionate morning kiss.

"I like that early in the morning," responded Kimoni.

"I can give you that whenever you like," Ming said as she kissed Kimoni again. "I have to go. I have a few things to take care of today."

"Okay, cool. Well, maybe we can get together later today."

"Sure, I will call you once I'm done or if you feel the urge, call me."

"Don't tempt me with an urge. I can find an urge," said Kimoni as she walked Ming to the door.

"Well, we can make that happen later," Ming said as she grabbed Kimoni's face and gave her a quick kiss good bye. "I'll call you later."

It was past noon when Ming left Kimoni's house. She was in disbelief about what had transpired. *Oh, man, what did I do*, she thought. *We had sex on the first date. No scratch that, we made love. I mean she made love to me like no one has ever done! Oh, what am I going to do? I wonder how she feels? Oh, what a wonderful night. It was great. No one has ever made love to me in that way.* The thoughts kept tumbling through her mind.

It had been so long since I have been with someone, but damn, did I have to give it up on the first date? Man, I need to tell someone. I have to tell someone. Whew, this woman has made my body feel like no other. I want some more I really want to get to know her too of all the women and all the people it had to be a stud that turned my head, Ming thought.

~

Kimoni was in heaven. *Oh, how Ming's body felt so damned good. These last few hours were better than she ever expected. Never did she think that she and Ming would become intimate so soon, but man she loved every fucking minute of it,* thought Kimoni.

Kimoni was at a loss for words. Ming had just left, but her scent was still strong on her sheets and pillows. *Mmm... she smells so good,* she thought as she closed her eyes to day dream about her night. Just then, her phone rang snapping her out of her trance.

Kimoni looked at her phone. She recognized the number instantly and thought, *why is she calling me? What could she possibly want? I don't even want to deal with that situation. You can leave a message,* Kimoni said to herself as she sent the call to voicemail.

CHAPTER EIGHTEEN

The sound of her doorbell woke Nayla from her slumber. *What time is it*, she thought to herself. She had wasted her whole day off cleaning her place and trying to get her mind off of PG. She must have fallen asleep because her laptop was still on the image of a sexy stud with a wife beater on was dancing around the screen. *Oh, how I love that screen saver*, she thought to herself. Her doorbell rang again, waking her from her trance.

"Just a minute! Here I come!" she called out. When Nayla opened the door, there was a messenger on her doorstep waiting for her. A fine assed, chocolate skinned stud.

"I have a package for a Miss Nayla Ivy," she said.

"Oh, that would be me," Nayla replied.

"Sign right here, ma'am."

Nayla signed the waiver on the clipboard and took the package.

"Thank you so much," she said to the messenger. "Have a nice day."

"You, too," answered the messenger as she turned and went down the stairs to get into her truck.

Hm…, I wonder what this is, she said to herself as she looked at the box. The box was beautiful with gorgeous wrapping. She picked up the note that was attached and began to read:

Dearest Nayla
If you enjoyed our time on the phone then you will love the night I have planned for us. Inside the box is what I need for you to wear. Be ready at 8 p.m.
PG

Nayla opened the box and could not believe her eyes. Inside was a black lace bra with a matching thong and a beautiful summer dress. *What the hell,* she thought. Nayla picked up the phone to call PG, but before she could dial the number, her phone rang.

"Hello," she said.

"Hello there beautiful," the voice on the other end greeted her.

"Hello, there you. I was just getting ready to call you."

"You were?" PG exclaimed. "So what happened to you calling me yesterday?"

"Oh, well, I kind of got a little busy and lost track of time," Nayla was lying. She couldn't call PG because she didn't know how to process what happened between them the day before.

"So are you calling because you needed to hear my voice on this wonderful Saturday morning?"

Nayla begin to chuckle, "No, I was calling you about the box…"

PG interrupted, "Yes?"

"What is this for?" she asked.

"Well, it's a surprise. Now, you can either trust me or you can decline my offer all together. It's up to you. Either way, you can keep the garments in the box. They are a gift. However, if you choose to trust me, then I promise to take you on one hell of a ride tonight."

"Really?" Nayla asked.

"Yes, really. So, are you game?"

Nayla thought to herself for a minute. *What was she getting into with PG? First, the other night and now, this.* "Mm… well, can you tell me what it entails?"

"No. Just know that you will be safe with me and I won't let anything happen to you."

"Oh, I know you won't," Nayla said. "Okay, I'll go with you. What time do you want me to be ready?"

"At 8," PG interjected.

"At 8," Nayla repeated. "So, now tell me how in the world did you get my address?"

"Oh, I have my ways," PG said with a chuckle. "So, I will pick you up tonight at 8. Don't worry about a thing."

"Okay, I won't. See you tonight," Nayla said and hung up the phone.

Oh my, she thought. *What am I doing? I don't trust myself around her. It was too late. She had already agreed to go out. Damn I need to call my girl,* she thought as she picked up the phone.

Nayla called Ming, but her phone went straight to voicemail.

"Shit," Nayla said aloud. *Who can I call I really need to talk to someone like right now. But who,* she thought, *I don't want to call Rachael or Angie.*

"Shit!" she said again out loud. Then she thought, *Kim. I will call Kim.* Nayla dialed Kim's number.

"Hello?"

"Hi, Kim, this is Nayla."

"Hey, what's up, Nayla? I know I was supposed to confirm the interview info with you, but I've been busy."

"No, no," said Nayla. "That's not what I'm calling you about."

"Then what?" asked Kim, confused.

"Well, I needed some advice," started Nayla.

"Advice? What kind?" Kim asked.

"Well, it's about a woman," replied Nayla. "I have some female problems, not some, but one in particular."

"Really?" Kim asked. "And you really think I should be the one giving you advice about some woman? Nayla, what the fuck? You broke my heart!"

"Come on, Kim," Nayla said. "That was a long time ago."

"Yes, it was, and, believe me, I am past it, but don't think for a minute that I have forgotten," Kim replied.

"I'm sorry, Kim. I just was…"

"I know. You just wasn't ready, but now you are and you have the nerve to call me to ask me advice on you being with another woman when you couldn't be with me? Come on, really? How about you do what you couldn't and didn't do with me and that's be honest about who you are? Nayla, you are a lesbian. Look in the mirror and face it," Kim said then hung up the phone in Nayla's face.

Nayla couldn't believe what had just happened. She looked at the phone in utter disbelief. She really needed to speak to someone quick. *What am I going to do? What do I really want to do,* she asked herself? *Damn, I do love pussy,* she thought to herself. But, there are two sides to the rainbow!

The fucking nerve of her. Like I am really going to be the one who she talks to about some other bitch. I don't think so. I don't call her ass for advice on women. But oh, I am out and proud and don't have to question that I am a fucking lesbian through and through! Just as Kim was about to toss her phone on the bed, her phone rang.

"WHAT!!" she answered thinking it was Nayla calling back.

"Good afternoon, Kim. It's Ray."

"Oh, hi, Ray. I'm so sorry. I thought you were someone else. I answered my phone without looking at the number."

"It's okay. I was calling to see if you had some time for me tonight. I would like to take you out."

"Sure, I do. I was hoping that you would call today. I was going to call you later to see if wanted to hang out."

"Well, would you look at that? Great minds do think alike."

"Well, I guess they do," Kim said.

"So, I will pick you up at 7p.m."

"Great, I will be ready. I will text you my home address."

"Okay, sounds good. Let me finish so that I will be straight when I pick you up."

"Yes, me too, and sorry again about how I answered the phone."

"It's okay. I'll let you make it up to me later."

"Okay, see you tonight," Kim said and they hung up the phone.

Kim texted Ray her home address and directions. She thought, *I am going to relax and enjoy myself tonight and not let anything or anyone stand in the way of that. It's been a long time since I enjoyed the company of a woman in more ways than one, and tonight just may be my night to have some fun.*

Against her better judgment, and cause she really needed to speak to someone, Nayla picked up the phone and called Rachael. As the phone rang, Nayla thought, *what am I doing? I am a grown woman. I don't need to speak to anyone.* Just as she was about to hang up, Rachael picked up.

"Hello?" she said.

"Hey, girl, what's going on with you?" Nayla asked.

"Nothing much. What about you?"

"Girl, getting ready to clean up. I guess I just thought I would call to see what you were up to."

"Nothing much. Oh, let me tell you. I ended up exchanging numbers with DC the other day."

"What?" Nayla exclaimed. "Now how in the hell did that happen? Did Ming give it to you?"

"Hell no, but I'm glad she didn't. It just so happened that DC had a photo shoot at my hotel the other day. And well, you know, I'm the total package and she couldn't resist."

"Really?" said Nayla.

"Well, of course, who can? But anyway, I was making my rounds and checking to see how everything was going and when I walked in my mouth almost dropped when I saw it was her. I thought, 'oh yes, she is on my turf let me work my charm.'"

"So, how did it go? Tell me. Don't leave anything out."

"Well, we talked briefly because we both were working."

"So, what did you talk about?"

"Nothing, really. She invited me to go out to dinner after her photo shoot."

"Did you go?"

"No, it was too late so we exchanged numbers so she could call me for us to have lunch."

"Oh, that's great. How did lunch go then?"

"It didn't go. She didn't call."

"Really? So, why didn't you call her?"

"Because, *she* is going to call me. I will never be the one to call first. Plus, she invited me, remember."

"So what. You want to have lunch don't you? Just give her a call!" Nayla said exasperated.

"Nope, I will wait until she calls me."

"Well, guess what, Miss Stuck Up? This is DC, the famous model. She may never call. Remember there are lesbians and a few, supposed to be, straight women lining up to be with her. And, you have the number and are too caught up in your crazy ways to call. Good luck with that one. Listen, let me call you back," Nayla said.

"Sure," replied Rachael and she hung up the phone.

Why did I ever think I would get some advice from her ass, thought Nayla when she hung up the phone.

Whatever, thought Rachael. *I will never call she is going to have to call me.*

DC had been busy with work the past couple of days and she hadn't called Rachael. She planned to, but she wanted to see if she would call her first. Most of the time, the ones who wanted something from her always tended to call first. They never wait to see if she would call. But, Rachael seemed different. In a way, she still gave off that vibe of 'I want all I can get,' but it was something else, too. She really wanted to get to know her without her stature being first.

Maybe I'll call her later on tonight to see where her head is at and that will determine what I will do next with her. DC headed out to go to the gym. I need to get my workout in and blow off some energy, especially if I'm going to call Rachael later. I don't want to have any sexual tension pinned up.

After working out and clearing her mind, DC decided to call Rachael to see if she would like to go out. Rachael didn't answer. DC hung up. She decided she wouldn't leave a message. *Maybe luck next time,* she thought. *Just as well, I need to stop and get something to eat and catch up with Kimoni. She hadn't been answering her phone either. I wonder what's up with that.*

CHAPTER NINETEEN

Ray arrived at Kim's place at exactly at 7 p.m. She rang Kim's doorbell and after a moment, the door opened and there stood Kim looking like a breath of fresh air.

"Hi, Ray, you're here. Come in. Let me get my purse and I will be ready."

"Okay," Ray replied as she walked into the foyer of Kim's home. "Nice place," she said as she looked around the corner to the living room.

"Thanks," Kim replied as she walked towards Ray. "Shall we go?"

Ray grabbed Kim's elbow and escorted her out of the door.

"So, where are we going tonight?" Kim asked Ray.

"Well, one of my friends is having an art exhibition and I wanted to take you with me to view it. You don't mind, do you?" she asked.

"Oh, no, not at all. That's cool. I love to see art and I really need to clear my mind."

"Well, maybe I can help you with that. Just relax and let me take care of you tonight. Your every wish is my command."

Upon arriving at the art gallery, they noticed it was starting to get a little crowded even though it was early. Ray pulled up front to the valet to park her car. Giving the keys to the parking attendant, she went around to Kim's side of the car and opened the door.

"Let me get that for you beautiful," she said. Ray took Kim by the arm and led her into the building. When they got inside, they were greeted with champagne and hors d'oeuvres.

"This is nice," Kim whispered to Ray.

"I'm glad you like it," she said as she handed Kim a glass of champagne from the waiter. "A toast. Let me just say, to new beginnings and new friendships."

"I will drink to that," Kim said as they struck their glasses together.

"Shall we?" Ray asked as she took Kim's elbow and escorted her around the gallery.

They stopped at a painting of wild flowers growing in a field. The painting had Kim's interest.

As they stood there looking at the piece, they began to engage in small talk.

"So, do you like this?" Ray asked.

"Yes, I do. It kind of reminds me of me."

"Really? Do tell," Ray said.

"Well, look. The flowers are beautiful, but they are in darkness, a field of nothing. They are alone, nothing else around, not even other flowers."

"Wow," Ray said. "I didn't look at it like that. I guess that's why they say art can be interpreted differently. Do you have a favorite flower?"

"Yes, lilies, I love them. The two stood looking at the painting for a moment longer before they continued to walk around the gallery and talk.

"So, tell me, if you don't mind me asking, what had you so upset this afternoon when I called?" Ray asked.

"Oh, it's nothing. Just a girl I used to mess with a long time ago."

"Oh, she trying to get you back?"

"No, nothing like that. She's actually someone I used to date a long time ago. We are still kind of friends, so to speak, but I was in love with her then and she wasn't ready to be in a lesbian relationship. One day, I poured my heart out to her and asked her to be with me in the open, because I wanted to stop sneaking around."

"So what happened?" Ray asked as she took Kim's hand.

"She told me no. Basically, she wasn't ready to come out of the closet and she was happy with living the lie that was our lives. But I wasn't. I was tired of pretending to just be her close friend. So, I left her that night and I haven't looked back."

"Wow! I'm sorry," Ray said as she kissed Kim's hand.

"Don't be sorry. It's her loss and, even now after all these years, she is still in the closet. She's the one that should be sorry. But enough about her, I'm here to enjoy my time with you. So, do tell, who do you know that made all this wonderful art work.

"Well, it's a very good friend of mine. Tell me, do you like."

"Of course, it's beautiful and I am really enjoying the time that I am spending with you."

"Good. Glad to hear it, because I am enjoying your company, as well. Shall we continue to look around and get something to eat from the buffet?"

"Sure," Kim said as they walked to the buffet to grab something to eat and find a table to enjoy their meal. After grabbing their dining selections, they sat down and chatted while they ate dinner.

"Oh, that was delish," Kim said as she finished her food.

"Yes, it was. So are you ready to see the rest of the artwork?"

"Yes," Kim said as they got up from the table and began to walk around to view remainder of the art show. "Oh, I am so tense," Kim stretched. "I hardly have time to do things like this. I miss just hanging out and being in the company of another woman."

"Do you?" Ray asked smiling. "Well, maybe now all that will change since I'm in the picture."

"Maybe it will," Kim replied smiling back maybe it will.

"Come on. Let me take you for a ride and clear your mind. The night air will do you good."

"Sure," Kim said. "I'm up for anything."

Ray and Kim rode around the city for a while just talking getting to know each other. They were laughing and having a good time.

"Hey, are you up for a surprise that could possibly relax you?"

"Sure, is it legal?" Kim said in an evil voice.

"Of course, it's legal, but if you want me to be illegal, I can arrange that," Ray laughed.

"No, no. I was just asking," Kim said laughing.

"Cool, then sit back, relax and enjoy the ride."

After riding around, they ended up going to Ray's place.

"Welcome to my humble abode."

"Nice and cozy. I like it," Kim said.

"Come on in and have a seat. Let me turn on some lights and music."

"Okay," Kim said as they continued to engage in small talk.

"I have a surprise for you."

"You do?" Kim said in a surprised voice. "Now what could it be?"

"Well I'm going to need for you to trust me and relax. I promise, I won't bite unless you want me to."

"Ha, ha! Don't tempt me. I just may ask you to bite me."

"And, I just may happily oblige. Come and sit here," Ray said as she took Kim by the hand. "Close your eyes and relax." Ray placed a blindfold over Kim's eyes.

"Don't take it off until I tell you to," Ray instructs as she left and went to her bedroom to get ready.

"Hey, Kim, are you ok?"

"Yes, Ray, I'm fine. Just waiting for you to come back with my surprise."

"Here I come. You are going to like it. Trust me," Ray said as she lit candles, turned off the lights and turned on some music. Johnny Gill's, In The Mood started to fill the room.

"I want you to listen to the words of this song, because I want you to know what I want from you."

"Take the blindfold off," Ray instructs Kim.

When Kim takes the blindfold off, Ray was standing in front of her dressed in a wife beater and baggy jeans. As the music played, Ray began to strip. She slowly moved her body to the music so seductively that Kim was being taken in with her every move.

Ray was great. She was rolling her body and taking off her clothes until she was standing in front of Kim with only her sports bra and boxer shorts.

Oh my, thought Kim. *What the fuck? Ray's body is off the chain.* Never before had anyone stripped for her. She was having a night that she would never forget.

Ray made her way closer to Kim. She began to kiss her gently. In and out, their tongues played with one another doing the seductive dances that Ray had just put on for Kim. Kim let her guard down and began to kiss Ray back. She wanted Ray just as bad as Ray wanted to get it and tonight she was going to give it up.

Fuck being careful and cautious. It never got her anywhere in the past and, tonight, she was going to experience everything that she could with Ray. It had been a long time since she had sex and now was the time for her to release all of the tension she had building up. Tonight, she felt as free as a bird.

After contemplating all day, Nayla decided she was just going to get ready and go out with PG. What's the worst that could happen, she thought. Nayla admired the gifts that PG had sent.

"Damn, this woman has good taste," she said out loud.

Nayla started to pace the floor, back and forth, her mind racing. *What am I going to do? Do I go? I don't even know this woman, but, whew, she makes me want to know her. Okay, I'm going,* she thought as she momentarily ceased the battle in her mind.

Nayla started her shower and got in. After taking a nice hot shower, she moisturized with scented oil. She wanted to look as well as her body felt and she wanted to smell delicious, she thought as she rubbed oil on her legs.

As she continued getting ready, she heard the text alert on her phone. She took a quick look and saw a text from PG.

Hey Nayla. It's PG. I'm sorry, but I'm going to have to take a rain check on our date tonight. Something came up.

What the fuck, Nayla thought. *Rain check? I just bet something came up. And she didn't even have the decency to call me in person. Who the fuck sends a text message? All that back and forth trying to decide if I was going to go and then she cancels anyway. Maybe I should call her and give her a piece of my mind. For what? I just decided I was going to go. Maybe she knew I really didn't want to come and she made it easy for me. Just as well.*

Nayla texted PG back a simple "OK."

Nayla wasn't sure how she should feel. She didn't know if should be happy or upset that she wasn't going out. One thing was for certain, she was curious to where they would have gone and what they would have done.

CHAPTER TWENTY

After an eventful night full of passion, lust and ecstasy, Ray and Kim fell asleep with Kim laying in Ray's arms. Ray held her tightly, not wanting to let her go. Ray awoke to the sun light breaking through her window panes, awakening her from the memorable night that she had just shared with Kim.

As Ray arose, she looked upon Kim's sleeping face. She was sound asleep and at peace. She looked wonderful with her long full eyelashes and soft, full lips that were just calling for Ray to kiss them. She knew if she did, it would start up an all day love feast, which wasn't a bad idea. But right now, she just wanted to reminisce on the events of last night. As Ray watched Kim sleep, she smiled and thought to herself, *damn!*

Ray got up to give Kim a special treat, which would be her on a platter again, but after what their bodies just shared, they needed to replenish with some nutrients. Ray went to the kitchen to whip up some breakfast.

The aroma of bacon, eggs, grits, and toast filled the air and Kim's nose, activating hunger pangs in her stomach which caused her to wake. She opened her eyes, stretched and scanned the room for Ray.

Their clothes were everywhere reminding her of the night of passion they just shared. Kim laughed to herself thinking of the naughty things she and Ray just engaged in. Her stomach rumbled again reminding her of why she woke up in the first place. Slowly, Kim made her way down Ray's stairs and into the kitchen. She turned the corner to find Ray cutting up fruit.

"What is all this? Is this for me?" she asked.

"Of course, baby. I have to keep you full of energy. You never know when I may need a little more of you," Ray replied.

Kim grabbed Ray by the waist and whispered in her ear, "You just may be getting more of me sooner than you think."

Ray chuckled and kissed Kim on the nape of her neck then swung her around to plant a wet, juicy kiss on her lips.

"I can't wait."

They stood there at the counter for what seemed like hours, kissing and kissing. They finally broke free and went to the table to eat their breakfast. While enjoying the food, they both fantasized about what the day would bring and blew kisses and made faces at one another until they finished eating.

When done, Kim got up to load the dishes in the dishwasher while Ray cleared the table. Kim thought how sweet, but Ray had something else in mind. Her appetite was not filled. She wanted more to eat and Kim was the dish she was looking forward to satisfying her craving.

Once she had the table cleared and clean, Ray took Kim by the hand and guided her back to the table. Ray made sure Kim was secure on top of the table then spread Kim's legs as if they were butter. Ray knelt and softly placed one kiss on Kim's love box.

A chill crept through Kim's body causing her to become excited and nervous all at the same time.

"Relax, baby, don't be afraid. I will take care of your every need."

Kim let her head go back as Ray ate, licked, and sucked the hell out of Kim's love box, as if there was no tomorrow.

Moaning in pure pleasure Kim called out, "How can you make my body feel this damn good?"

Ray's tongue found its home in Kim's love box making sure she could feel every stroke of it. Kim's pink muscle couldn't get enough of Ray's tongue. With the last stroke of Ray's tongue, Kim found her way to ecstasy. All of her juices filled Ray's throat. Ray swallowed as she placed light kisses on Kim's wet pussy.

"Damn, baby, you taste so good. I could eat you for breakfast, lunch and dinner any day."

Kim smiled, for that's exactly what she wanted to hear. Ray took Kim's hand and helped her to sit up straight then she helped Kim down off the table.

With Ray's hands still around her waist, Kim looked into Ray's eyes and said, "Who knew breakfast could feel so good."

They laughed and shared a passionate kiss.

Rachael woke up feeling refreshed after spending all day at the spa thinking about whether or not she should call DC. The spa was wonderful. She got the works: full body massage, facial, mud bath, waxing, manicure and pedicure. What else could a girl do besides shopping to pamper herself for the day?

Rachel stretched, got out of bed and went to the bathroom to brush her teeth and wash her face. As she looked in the mirror, she admired her good looks then blew herself a kiss.

When she was done in the bathroom, Rachael walked into the kitchen and began making breakfast. Even though it was almost 12 in the afternoon, she made herself waffles and scrambled egg whites. As she was pouring her orange juice into a glass, her phone rang.

"Hello?"

"Hello there. Is this Ms. Rachael?"

"Yes, it is and whom may this be?"

"Hi, this is DC."

"Hello, DC. How are you? How have you been?"

"I've been good. Thanks for asking. I'm sorry that I didn't get a chance to call you. Things have been kind of hectic."

"It's ok. I know you are a very busy woman. I'm glad that you called now."

"Well, actually, I did call you yesterday, but you didn't answer so I figured you were busy."

"Oh, you called me yesterday? I am so sorry. I was out for a pamper day."

"Really, what's a pamper day?"

"A pamper day is when I treat myself to the spa for the entire day and I get the works from waxing to facial. Oh, wow, was that too much information?"

"No, no, that's cool. Sounds like fun. I love to get massages."

"I got one of those, too. I am so relaxed. I'm so glad I went because it took away so much stress."

"Well, I'm glad you had a spa day. It's good to know that you are a woman who takes care of herself."

"Oh, yes, that is a must. So, tell me, DC, how is it being a mega model?"

"Oh, its fine. Just fine."

"It couldn't be just fine. Having anything at your disposal must be great. From fine women, to cars, wine, food, the works, do you feel like you have it all?"

"Well, to be honest, yes and no. It's kind of complicated. All in all, it has it ups and downs, but I can't complain. Over all, I am blessed."

"That you are. I must say you were looking real good at the photo shoot."

"Thank you, thank you. So you liked?"

"Yes, I did. I must admit, but hey, you are used to that, I'm sure."

"Yeah, I am. I can have anything that I want, but it's what I choose that matters, not what chooses me."

"I'm sure," Rachael replied with a chuckle.

"What's the laugh for?" DC asked.

"Nothing, I just know that you have everything and for me I wouldn't mind knowing what that's like."

"Really?" DC asked. "You want the fame, huh?"

"Well, being able to provide for yourself and not want for nothing is something I think everyone wants, but to be honest, I would love to be in your shoes. I love the finer things in life and to have your kind of stature would make me happy."

"Wow, go figure. I didn't think you would be so blunt."

"No, no, no disrespect. I'm just saying being in your position puts so many things at your fingertips. Things that most people will never be able to experience."

"You're right, but there is also a down side to this."

"Down side? What could that possibly be?"

"Well, Miss Lady, you will just have to take my word for it. This industry can eat you up and spit you out. I am thankful for what I have been blessed with."

"My, you are very humble. I never expected that, you know, most models are so… so, vain."

"Girl, you are something else, I tell you. Are you calling me stuck up?"

"No, I am so sorry. I have just been putting my foot in my mouth this whole conversation, haven't I?"

"Yes, you have," DC laughed as a call came in on her phone. "Hey, Rachael, can you hold on a moment? I have another call coming in."

"Sure," Rachael said.

"Hello?" DC said when she clicked over.

"Hey, man, what's up? I see you called me a few times. I was returning your call. What's going on?"

"Nothing much. On the phone, right now. Can I hit you back?"

"Yeah, man."

DC clicked back over to Rachael, "Sorry about that, now where were we?"

After she finished talking to Rachael, DC called Kimoni back.

"Hey man, what's the business?"

"Nothing much," Kimoni replied. "Just flipping through the TV channels."

"Hey, man, let's go play one on one. You game?"

"Hell yeah. I need to kick your ass in some b-ball."

"Whatever, man, if you think you can handle it, come and get it. I will meet you on the court in 30 minutes. Don't be late."

"Oh no, bro, make sure you're there so you can get this ass whipping."

~

Kimoni parked her car at the court and began to contemplate whether or not she should tell DC about what transpired between her and Ms. Foster. She couldn't get the events out of her mind. Never before had she experienced such ecstasy.

Kimoni had been with her share of women, but something about Ming set her apart from any other.

Never mind the fact that she was so sophisticated and elegant, her sex, or should she say love making, was off the charts. But, Kimoni wasn't the type to kiss and tell, so she would just keep it to herself for now.

It all happened so quickly and she was happy that it had. Hell, it was so fucking good. *Damn*, she thought, *I have to say something. I need to tell someone. DC is my boy, she will understand.*

DC was shooting free throws when Kimoni walked up. "Hey, man."

"Hey, what's up?" DC replied as she stopped taking shots. She walked over to Kimoni and gave her dap. "Hey are you ready for this ass kicking?"

"Are you still on that?" Kimoni asked. "You must be ready for me to take you to school."

"School?" DC said as they walked back onto the court. "Yeah, alright, let's see. I'm going to kick your ass so good that I'm going to give you the ball first." DC bounced the ball to Kimoni.

"Oh, okay, you don't want to score any points. Cool by me." They both started to laugh and the games began.

As they battled on the court, they began a conversation.

"Hey man, where were you? What's been going on? I've been calling you."

Kimoni hit the jumpshot with ease. "Yeah, I know. I was kinda busy."

"Busy? You must have been with La'Ming Foster," DC said as she dribbled the ball then went to make a layup. "So, how did it go?"

"Man, it went wonderfully."

"Hm… with that smile on your face it looks like it went a little bit more than wonderfully."

"Uh huh," Kimoni chuckled. "Yeah, man, is all I can say. But enough about me. What about you? Who was you on the phone with earlier?"

"Oh, man, while you were hanging out with Ms. Foster, remember her friend I told you about?" DC replied as she shot the ball.

"Yeah, what about her?"

"Well, turns out she works at the hotel where I had the photo shoot last week."

"Get the fuck outta here! Talk about a small world."

"I know, right man."

"Well how did it go? You were talking about how you wanted to meet her. So, you got the chance, what happened?"

"Nothing, really. We were just talking. Maybe we will get together sometime this week."

"For sure. I think Ming and I will be having dinner one day this week, too."

"Well, will you look at us? Things have really started to come together."

"I second that motion," Kimoni said as they continued their game.

CHAPTER TWENTY ONE

Kimoni had left Ming a voicemail message before she left to play ball with DC. In the message, she said:

Hello there, sweetie. I just wanted to let you know that you are in my thoughts. I will try to reach you later. Talk with you soon, bye.

Kimoni left to play ball immediately after leaving the message.

Ming didn't hear the phone ring, but she received the alert that she had missed a call. She saw that it was from Kimoni and checked the message. She listened to the message and smiled. *She is so wonderful*, she thought as she called Nayla.

Nayla picked up the phone immediately.

"Hey, girl, what is going on? I have been trying to call you for a minute. What have you been doing?"

"Girl, you won't believe me if I told you, but hey, what's up? What was so urgent?"

"I have to talk to you face to face."

"Okay, come on over now, I'm just chillin'. I don't feel like going to the gym today."

"Okay, I'm on my way," Nayla said then hung up the phone.

Nayla got to Ming's house quickly. She ran up Ming's stairs and rang her doorbell.

"Hey you," Ming said as she opened the door. "Come on in the back. Lock the door behind you, please."

"Okay, girl, what the hell are you doing in the back?" When Nayla got in the back Ming was doing her laundry. "Laundry? I'm surprised you're doing that today."

"You can help me fold these towels."

"I came over here to talk to you not help you fold your towels."

"Whatever, you can kill two birds with one stone, babe. So, what's wrong?"

"Well, the other day I received a gift from PG."

"Really? What kind of gift?"

"Well, it was a beautifully wrapped box and inside was a black, lace underwear set along with a summer dress."

"What?" Ming exclaimed. "Why did she send you some undergarments? I gotta admit, that's some sexy ass shit, but I guess she wanted to see you in it and then take it off of you, right? Tell me, girl, give me the dirt."

"I guess," Nayla said. "There isn't any dirt. I didn't get a chance to wear anything. We were supposed to go out the night she sent the package, but at the last minute, she canceled on me."

"Really? I wonder why?" Ming mused.

"I don't know, but that's not even the half of it. I really didn't know if I wanted to go. I had agreed to go but then I started having doubts."

"Why? Did you call her back and tell her you didn't want to go?"

"No, I didn't. I called to talk to you, but you were tied up and shit," Nayla said laughing. "And then, girl, get this. I called Kim."

"Kim?" Ming asked with a surprised look on her face. "Why?"

"I don't even know. Shit, I needed someone to talk to."

"And you thought she was the person to speak to?"

"Yeah, because I couldn't get in touch with your ass so, hell, I called her."

"And how did that go?"

"Well, she went off on me."

"I just bet she did," Ming said laughing. "She went off right after you told her what it was about didn't she?"

"Yeah, she did. How did you know?"

"Because, Nayla, she was in love with you and you let her go because you were, no, you are, too scared to be true."

"But, shit, Ming, how long ago was that?"

"It doesn't matter, Nayla. You know how lesbian love can be. Oh, wait, you act like you don't since you want to pretend that you are not a lesbian."

"Whatever, Ming," Nayla said.
"It's the truth and when you start facing the truth then things will get better."

"Ming, I don't need to hear that shit! I am who I am, period!"

"Who you are," Ming replied, "is a lesbian that is in denial! You need to fucking face your fears!" Ming took Nayla's face in her hands and looked into her eyes. "I love you, babe, no matter who or what you are, but you need to know and understand you are never going to be happy living a life that is a lie."

A tear ran down Nayla's face and she didn't say a word. She just hugged her friend, tightly.

"I'm not trying to be mean to you. I just want you to be happy and know that being happy doesn't mean living your life the way someone else wants you to. You only have one life to live and when it's over, it's done. Please, baby, if you don't want to listen to me, listen to your heart. It won't steer you wrong. I'm your best friend and I want nothing but happiness for you at all times."

"I know," Nayla said. "You just don't understand. It's not as easy for me to just come out or just be open with my family."

"I care about you, period." Ming interrupted.
"I know you do and thank you for being a friend and giving me your views. Trust and believe I hear you. I do!" Nayla gave Ming another hug.

"Thanks for everything, but I'm getting ready to go home so I can get ready for work. I'll call you tomorrow."

"Sure thing. Let me walk you to the door." As they walked to the door Ming wondered if she was being too hard on her friend. "Hey, Peanut, remember that I love you, but it's time that you start loving yourself."

"I know and I'm going to start doing just that. I love you too, Ming, and thanks again for being here. It means the world to me."

"I will always be here," Ming replied as she gave Nayla a hug good bye and closed the door.

~

On her drive home, Nayla knew she had some soul searching to do. She just didn't want to face what was clearly in front of her. She decided she would just throw herself into her work and nothing else, because as the old saying goes, out of sight out of mind.

The first thing I need to do is call Kim and apologize to her about what happened, she thought. *No, I won't call. I will go see her first thing in the morning. I need to get the*

*information about DC's interview, anyway. We can discuss
everything then.*

When Nayla made it home, she was mentally
exhausted. She just wanted to take a long hot bath
and go to bed. She ran her bath water and added bath
salts and bubbles so that she could relax more quickly.
As Nayla got undressed to get into the tub, she looked
at herself in the mirror.

"Who am I?" she asked herself out loud. "Why
can't I be true to myself? Please, I need to."

Nayla got in the tub and tried to relax. She laid
in the tub soaking and trying to de-stress. The hot
water felt so good. Nayla tried to block out her earlier
conversation with Ming earlier. She didn't want to
think about it or address it in this moment. Instead,
she let her mind wander to the day her mom caught
her and her best friend. That's the day that changed
her life, dramatically.

The first time she kissed a girl was when her and
her best friend, Karen, were under the covers playing
house. That time was innocent enough. I was the
mom and Karen was the dad. After all, all mom and
dad's kiss. It was just so natural. My mom asked
what we girls were doing and we both said nothing.
We quickly picked up our dolls and returned to
playing with them. Throughout the years, Karen and I

would experiment every chance we got. Our first kiss was when we were eight years old and it continued throughout our teenage years. Then it all came to an end. Our friendship was over.

One Friday night, Karen was at my house for one of our usual sleepovers. This time we were home alone. It was the perfect time. We wanted to go all the way. We both had grown tired of just kissing and fondling. We wanted more. So, we decided we would make love to each other the best we could. We would do whatever came natural to us. So, we did and it was wonderful. Just as I finished going down on Karen and we began to tongue kiss, in walks my mom.

For a minute neither one of us noticed her standing there in disbelief. Then all I remember is my mom yelling and screaming my name. Cursing, using words I had never heard her say before. I had never seen my mom so angry.

How could she be mad, I thought, *I was happy and in love with Karen.* This was so right. Wrong. My mom made us get dressed and she called Karen's mother to come and pick her up. I remember her on the phone with her saying, 'you need to get here right away because I just caught them doing the unthinkable.'

The next thing I know, Karen's mom was there and she was screaming just as loud as my mom. 'How could you,' they asked us? 'What the hell are you two doing?' 'That is nasty and unclean' were some of the things they said to us.

Both of us sat there with tears streaming down our faces. We didn't understand why it was so wrong when it felt so right. That was the last night I would ever see Karen again.

My mom was so upset that she didn't speak to me for the entire weekend. It wasn't until Sunday morning on our way to church that she said, 'you don't ever have to worry about having those feelings again. You will be getting prayer for those feelings and they will all go away.'

Go away? How could this go away, I thought to myself. There I sat, a 16 year old, not knowing what was going to happen next.

After the church service, my mom rushed me into one of the church offices and there stood the pastor and some deacons. All of whom were telling me to not be afraid. They said they were going to cast the spirit out of me.

Next thing I knew, they were all praying, yelling, and laying hands on me. After about an hour of back and forth and them taking turns praying and telling me to receive it and let go, the pastor announced that

I would no longer have those feelings. They were wrong.

I never understood what they were trying to do and why. I didn't understand what made them think that putting me in a room full of praying adults would stop the feelings that I had on the inside.

Once they were done, my mom left out of the room with the other adults to speak to the pastor. When she came back in, she said to me, 'it's over and done, so you need to pack those feelings away.' Her next words were 'let's go.'

Once we left that room of the church, we never spoke of that day again and my mom never addressed the issue of me possibly being gay. There I sat in the car on the way home. I was a 16 year old who knew that the feelings I had would never go away. I loved girls. I always did, always have and always will.

Nayla got out of the tub not feeling any better than she did before she got in. The morning always looks brighter, she thought to herself. Nayla got into bed with a heavy heart. Not knowing which way to go, she began her nightly prayers. She hoped that they would ease her pain.

"Please give me direction," she pleaded aloud as she turned off the light on her nightstand.

CHAPTER TWENTY TWO

Kim could not believe the weekend was over so quickly. *Damn*, she thought to herself as her alarm went off. *Is it Monday already? Oh, how I want to rewind time back to Saturday and spend a few more hours with Ray*, she thought.

Kim's phone began to ring. It was Ray. "Hello," she said.

"Why, hello there, sexy. How are you this morning?"

"I'm good. What about you?"

"I'm doing better now that I've talked to you."

Laughing Kim replied, "Oh, really? Well, that's good to hear. What are you doing later on today?"

"Nothing, just working. I have a lot of things to handle that I didn't take care of this weekend. But, the most important thing that I needed to take care of this weekend, I managed to handle," Ray said seductively.

"Stop it, Ray, you're making me blush."

"Oh, I want to make you do more than that."

"And I certainly wouldn't stop you," Kim replied as they both started to laugh.

"Well, babe, I just wanted to touch base with you this morning. I know once you get to work, it'll be a wrap and I won't be able to talk to you unless I call in to your show and talk dirty to you. Would you like that?" Ray asked.

"Don't temp me. I would have my engineer put you straight through."

"I know. You have a good show tonight and I'll talk with you soon. Text me if you can."

"Okay," Kim said and hung up the phone.

Kim was on top of the world this morning. She had spent the weekend with a fine ass stud that made love to her body like no other had. Whatever this high was, she didn't want to come down from it and she was determined not to let anyone fuck it up either.

Kim got out of the bed, fixed herself a quick breakfast and got ready for work. At her usual time, she headed out of the house. It was time to make that dough.

When she arrived at the radio station, everyone seemed to be all smiles. Everyone was saying hello as she passed them by. She replied to every single one of them. Intrigued, she thought, *I wonder why everyone is all smiles today?* Just as she was walking down the hall past her producer's office, her producer came out and started walking with her.

"What did you do this weekend?" she asked.

"Why do you ask?" Kim was evasive. "A little of this and a little of that, why?"

"Just asking," she said. "See you in a minute."

"Okay," Kim replied as she continued to walk down the hall to her office.

She opened the door and couldn't believe her eyes. For on her desk was a big, beautiful bouquet of lilies.

"Oh, my God," she gasped as she walked to her desk, picked up the card and began to read:

> *To no more feeling alone with no one around,*
> *for I am here to fill that void of darkness,*
> *for you are as beautiful as these flowers, enjoy.*
> *Sincerely*
> *Ray*

Oh my goodness, thought Kim. *She remembered what I said at the gallery.*

"Wow," she said aloud.

"Wow, what?" asked her producer, Connie, as she entered the room. "Beautiful flowers. I guess a wow is in order. That's why everyone is all smiles around here, huh?"

"Well, I guess so," Kim replied without giving any details about whom the flowers were from. Kim didn't get down with talking her personal business at work. Kim believed work is for just that, work.

"Well, I guess you aren't going to give away any information about who sent them, are you?" Connie asked.

"Nope," Kim replied as she put the card in her purse. "I'm getting ready for the show. So tell me what's on our agenda for tonight."

Connie began to talk business with Kim about the show's format for the evening. Once Connie was done, Kim called Ray.

"Hi, you, I got the flowers. Thank you so much. I love them."

"You're very welcome," Ray replied. "I just wanted to put a smile on your face while you were working."

"Well, you did just that. Mission accomplished."

"I'm glad that you like."

"Yes, I do. I just had to call you really quickly and let you know, but I'll call you later on tonight."

"Okay, I'll talk with you later," Ray replied and hung up the phone.

Oh wee, Kim thought.

~

Kim was smiling from ear to ear when she heard a knock at her door.

"Come in," she said as she put her cell phone away. She was surprised to see that the person knocking was Nayla.

"Hello, Kim."

"Hello, what can I do for you?" Kim said in a very dry voice.

"Well, I'm here for two things. The first is to apologize for this weekend."

"Okay, I'm listening."

"I just want you to know that I recognize that I was insensitive to your feelings when I called you. No matter how long it's been between us, I should have known better then to call you for advice about another woman."

"You're fucking right! You shouldn't have! What do I look like telling you how to be with a woman when I wanted you to be with me for so long? Even though I don't care anymore, I am not going to be the one to tell you if you should be with someone. Hell, you couldn't be with me and I loved you with all that I was."

"I know. I know. That's why I came here today, to apologize for my behavior and let you know I was wrong. Whatever I need to do about that situation, I need to figure it out on my own."

"Yes, you do," Kim replied. "Look, Nayla, don't get me wrong, I want you to be happy just like I want myself to be happy. I realized a long time ago that you and I would never be happy together so it's not about you being with me. It's about you knowing." Kim took Nayla's face in her hands and said, "I was the first woman to ever love you mind, body and soul, sweetie."

Tears filled Nayla's eyes. "I know that. I do. I just…"

"I know you couldn't give me what I needed and I get that. So, now, that's the past and we are in the present and the future has not come. So, if you look hard enough inside of you, you may take a stand and become the woman that you already know to be without calling and asking anyone for their approval."

Kim handed Nayla a box of Kleenex to wipe her eyes. "Yes, I know. I'm working towards that, really I am." Nayla said as she wiped her eyes

"Good to hear. Now, come give me a hug. You will come into your own. It takes some longer than others," Kim said as she pulled Nayla into a tight embrace.

Finally, this was the closure that they both needed for their personal relationship. After a few moments, they both composed themselves and continued their business.

"Okay, the second thing I am wondering about is if you know when you will be able to fit DC in a slot for your show?" Nayla asked.

"Well, not at the moment. I am waiting on the programming director. Once I find out what's available I will call or text you."

"Okay, sounds good," Nayla said. "I'll see you later." Just as she was about walk out the door she turned around and said, "Thank you again, Kim, for loving me even after all I put you through."

Kim looked at Nayla with tears in her eyes and replied, "That's what lesbians do. We love hard."

~

Kim sat there for a minute to reflect on the turbulence that had been Nayla. She was finally able to set her free. Even though many years had passed since they first met and began their relationship, she still had a love for her in her heart.

She sighed heavily. She felt like a weight had been lifted. She was glad that the chapter that was Nayla was over in her life. She was on to better things now. No more pretending that the demands of her job were the reason she couldn't or wouldn't date. The real reason was she didn't want to be hurt or let down. So, she protected her feelings from everything and everyone.

Throughout the whole show, Kim's mind was on Ray. She couldn't get her and their weekend out of her mind. She kept having flash backs of Ray dancing for her. Laughing to herself, she thought Ray was certainly something and she was someone Kim wanted to keep in her life.

Right before the show ended Kim sent Ray a text letting her know she was on her mind and that she was thinking about the wonderful weekend they shared. She couldn't wait to get home to call and talk to Ray. She looked forward to what their upcoming conversation.

When Kim got home, she put her beautiful flowers on the kitchen table. The scent from the flowers filled the room. Kim still couldn't believe what had transpired over the last 48 hours. *Damn*, she thought to herself, *now this is how a woman is supposed to be treated. I'm going to do something real special for Ray, but what*, she thought. She was going to have to find out what Ray really liked.

Kim began to undress. She turned on the water to fill the tub for a bath then turned on her favorite jazz CD, which was a mixture of John Coltrane, Miles Davis and Charlie Parker. "I just want to fall out," she said to herself, "but only after I speak with Ray. Only then will I truly get a good night sleep."

Once Kim was done with her bath she picked up the phone and dialed Ray's number.

CHAPTER TWENTY THREE

Nayla went to see Ming after she left Kim's office. She wanted to get an idea of DC's availability and get the on air interview scheduled.

"Hey ya, girl," Angie said as Nayla walked in.

"Hello there, my dear."

"What's going on wit cha?"

"Nothing much. Just here to get some dates squared away with Ming, that's all. What are you doing later?"

"Oh, nothing much. Why, what's up?"

"Nothing. Just asking what was up."

"Okay, cool," Angie said. "Do you have plans?"

"Girl, who knows. I don't have any plans, but by the end of the day, that could change" Nayla laughed.

"I know that's right," Angie replied. "That's how I do shit day by day. I may run some errands later on, though."

"Okay," Nayla said. "Can you call and see if Ming is busy or if I can come in now."

"Okay, yeah, I forgot that you were coming to see her," Angie said as they both started laughing. Angie picked up the telephone to inform Ming that Nayla was on her way in.

~

"Hey, babe," Nayla said as she walked into Ming's office. "What's the business?"

"Nothing much," Ming responded, "and why have I been blessed with your presence today?"

"Because I was, just spreading cheer to those who need it," said Nayla jokingly.

"Whatever, I have a whole lotta cheer," Ming replied. "You either need something or you want to talk, so spill it."

"Oh, you have so little faith in me my best friend. I was actually coming to check DC's schedule. I want to get her radio interview confirmed."

"Okay, yes, I have her schedule here, I think," Ming said as she looked through a file to find DC's schedule. "Hey, let me call her business manager and get it faxed to me to make sure. I can't seem to find her itinerary. I know that you are working hard for me to get this interview done and, thanks, because you don't have to do that."

"I know, but its okay. You are my best friend and I will do anything for you."

"I know and I feel the same," Ming replied. "Let me get on top of getting you a secure date for the interview."

"Thanks, Ming. You're the best. Hey, let me go. I have some errands to run and not enough time."

"Okay, boo, love ya. I'll call you tonight when I get off."

~

When Nayla left Ming's office, she went straight to her office. She needed to get to work on the article for PG's clothing store. She hadn't spoken directly to PG since she invited her out the other night and she hadn't had any contact since she left her that text message. But, if she needed to contact her, it would be for business reasons only. She needed to be professional at all times with her, even though PG brought out something in her that she just couldn't explain. *Damn*, she thought.

When Nayla arrived at work, she went to the photography department to see who was available to take pictures of PG.

"Hey, Mark," she said as she walked into the room.

"Hey there, Miss Thang, how are you?"

"I'm good. I wanted to know if you could go take some pics of an owner and her place of business for an article."

"Sure, honey. When do you need me to take care of it? I'm not scheduled to anything right now but you know how that can change."

"Yes, I do, and that's why I'm asking you now instead of setting up the appointment the other way. I am getting ready to contact the person now and I will let you know in about an hour."

"Okay, sounds good, sweetie."

Mark was a photographer that worked for the magazine. He was a joy to be around and great at his job.

When Nayla got to her desk, she called PG at the store. She wanted to get Mark scheduled to come by and shoot the pictures.

"Thank you for calling Frames. How can I help you?"

"Hi, is Ms. Glover available? This is Nayla Ivy calling from Out and About Magazine."

"Yes, just one moment."

Nayla held the phone wondering how PG would respond. Would she bring up their broken date or would she just be professional and not say anything at all?

"This is Ms. Glover. How may I help you?" PG said as she got on the line.

"Hi, PG, this is Nayla. How are you?"

"I'm fine, Ms. Nayla. How are you doing today?"

"I'm good. I was calling because I need to schedule a date and time to have my photographer come by and take photographs of you and the store for the article."

"Oh, yes, that's right. Let me look at my calendar. It seems as though next Friday at 12 would be good."

"Okay, sounds good. I am adding you for that time. The photographer's name is Mark Woodson. I will let him, and his crew, know your schedule."

"Okay, Ms. Ivy, now that business is done, let me just apologize for the other night. Something came up and I wasn't able to get out of it."

"It's okay, PG, I understand."

"Well, I'm glad that you do because I'm going to make it up to you this weekend and I don't want to hear no if ands or butts about it. I'm still going to need for you to wear what I sent to you in the box. Can you do that for me?"

"Hm… let me see what I can do about that."

"Okay, okay, you work that out. I am going to call you later this evening if I can. If not, you keep it sweet. Okay?"

"Yeah, okay, I will, PG," Nayla said laughing. "I will talk to you soon," she said as they hung up the phone.

Nayla couldn't help but laugh about what PG just said. What was it about this woman that had her so fucking open? She couldn't put her finger on it, but she wanted to find out what PG was about.

She couldn't wait to get home. She was exhausted mentally and she just needed to relax. She knew that Ming was going to call her when she got home and she wanted to be in the bed and watching T.V.

Ming had just finished up everything she needed to do for the day when she called Angie into her office. Hey, Ang, come in here for a moment please."

"Okay, boss lady, I'm on my way."

When Angie arrived in her office, they talked business for a moment and then they started to chat.

"So, girl, what's been up with you lately?" Ming asked.

"Shit, nothing, just a little bit of this and a little bit of that. What about you?"

"Same here. Nothing much going on. Just wanted to check in with you. We haven't gotten together so I wanted to check on my girl," Ming said.

"Why thank you, boss lady. You know I love ya."

"I love you, too," Ming said giving Angie an imaginary kiss.

"Well, Ming, I'm about to call it a night. I'm done for the day and I have to go to the grocery store because my cabinets are suffering. They need to be feed and so do I."

Ming started to laugh, "Girl, you crazy. I need to pick up some things, too. I guess I could go with you."

"That would be great because I didn't drive today. I was dropped off."

"I bet you were," Ming laughed.

They left work and drove to the grocery store.

"Hey, I'm going to only get a few items. I don't feel like putting up a lot food tonight."

"I feel you. I'm only picking up some stuff for the next couple of days, that's it that's all."

As the ladies walked around the grocery store, they chatted about what was going on in their lives.

"Ming, I met this stud and, you know, she seems really cool, but she isn't giving me the time of day, at all." Angie confessed

"Really? Why?" asked Ming

"I don't know. I met her in passing, so to speak, and every time we meet, it's in passing. I would like to get to know her a little bit, but she just isn't having it."

"Well, baby, you can come on a little strong."

"Strong?" Angie repeated.

"Yes. Strong. You have to know when to step back and let the stud take control. You are a control freak and like to be in the driver's seat at all times. Maybe this stud wants someone who is less aggressive and more laid back."

"Maybe so, but I'm not going to stop being me just to get with a woman."

"No, no, no, that's not what I'm saying. All I'm saying is try not to be so direct. Sit back and relax and let them take control. It's not that hard, trust me."

"Oh, really? You don't even date studs so why should I even listen to you?"

"Well, that may change," Ming replied.

"Whatever, honey. You will never date a stud. You said so yourself. What's making you change your mind? Did you meet a stud? Oh, do tell, Ms. Hot Thang!"

"Well, it's nothing to tell. What are you talking about?" Ming asked.

"Come on, bitch. I know you. We have been friends for a long time and you giving me advise on studs? What stud pulled your chain?"

Just as Ming was getting ready to answer Angie, a voice from behind interrupted them.

"Excuse me, beautiful ladies," the voice said.

"Oh, pardon us. We were just talking," Ming said as she looked at the stud that had walked up behind them.

"It's okay. I just wanted to grab something off the shelf right there."

Both Ming and Angie moved out of the stud's way so that she could get her item.

"You ladies have a nice evening."

"You do too," Angie replied. Then turned to Ming. "Oh wee, girl, damn. This city knows it has some fine ass women."

"Yes, it does," Ming replied. "Come on. Are you ready?"

"Yes, I am done. Let's go check out.

They went to the front of the store and checked out with their groceries. As they exited the story, Stony walked in.

"Well, hello there you," Angie said to Stony.

"Ms. Angie, I'm starting to think you're following me," she said with a grin.

"Oh no, baby, if I was going to follow you, it would have been to your home," Angie said with a laugh.

"Oh, really? You are too much."

"That I am," Angie said. "That I am. We just keep running into one another. Maybe it's a sign."

"A sign? What kind of sign?" Stony teased.

"That we need to get to know each other. What are the odds?"

"I don't know, but our paths do keep crossing, don't they?"
"Yes, they do. So, maybe the stars are trying to tell us something. Oh, where are my manners? This is Ming. Ming, this is Stony."

"How do you do?" they both said in unison.

"I won't keep you, but know that if we run into each other again then we are going to have to go on a date," Angie said as she winked at Stony.

"You are too much for me. Nice meeting you, Ming. Have a good evening, ladies," Stony said as she walked away.

"Who was that?" Ming asked as they walked to the car.

"That's the stud I was just talking about in the store."

"Get the fuck outta here!"

"Yes, we keep running into each other and, man, I want to get to know her a little better."

"I just bet you do," Ming said.

"No, I'm serious. She seems hella cool. And, like I said, I'm interested in getting to know her."

"Well, she's fine as fuck and good luck with that, because she looks like she is going to be a tough nut to crack," Ming said as she closed the trunk of her car.

"I know," Angie said as they got inside the car. "That's what I mean. I don't know what to do. I'm not looking to get married, you know. I just want to…"

"Have fun," Ming finished.

"Well, yeah, kinda."

"But, maybe she's not that one who wants to have fun. Maybe she knows that you just want to kick it and not be serious. Have you ever thought about that?"

"Well, no, because it's always been me kicking it and doing what I do. I haven't had time for a relationship. You know that."

"Baby, everybody isn't on that "I'm kicking it thang" and it just maybe getting a little old."

"Maybe you're right. I need to reevaluate some things in my life right now."

"Yeah, perhaps," Ming said as they arrived at Angie's house.

"Thank you so much. That's why I love you," Angie said as they carried the groceries into her house.

"Okay, that will be $50," Ming laughed.

"$50 for what?"

"Well, that will be transportation there and back. Then it's the bringing of your groceries into the home and the filing fee."

"Filing fee? Girl, get the hell out of here! I love you, Ming," Angie said.

"I love you back," Ming said as they shared a quick hug and kiss on the cheek. "See you tomorrow."

"Will do, boss lady. Bye," Angie said as she walked Ming to the front and watched her get into her car.

Angie watched her drive away before she closed the door. *That woman is crazy*, she thought to herself. As she put her groceries away, she wondered what she needed to do to get Stony's attention. She thought she should just step back and not even pursue her since it seemed like she was coming off so strong.

Angie fixed herself something to eat and turned on the T.V. She thought about what it was she wanted and how she needed to change some things. Out with the old and in with the new, she thought.

CHAPTER TWENTY FOUR

Ming couldn't wait to get home and open a bottle of wine. She needed to relax. She had so much on her mind. She was worried about her friend Nayla and the stress of not being able to come out of the closet might be taking a toll on her.

She wanted to help but it wasn't her fight. Nayla had to find the strength in herself to overcome it. She would be there for her friend, no matter what she needed, night or day. Because coming out, and being true to yourself, is a very difficult thing to do when you don't have the support that you need. Family and friends can be so cruel. People fear what they don't understand.

It is a shame how being true to whom you are will cost you to lose your loved ones. But in the end, no matter what the situation, you and only you have to live your life. No one else can do it for you.

Ming thanked God that she had the courage to stand up, but there were so many that didn't and they didn't have anywhere to turn. Being supportive is the best thing she could do for Nayla, right now. She could just be that ear she needed.

Once she got home, Ming put her groceries away and then put on a pot of tea. She decided against the wine. She just wanted to eat a light dinner and have some tea then curl up with her book. Ming began to grill a chicken breast to go on top of a salad when her cell phone rang. It was Kimoni.

"Hello," Ming answered.

"Hello, sweetness. How are you this evening," Kimoni said.

"I'm well, thank you, but even better now that you've called. How are you doing?" she asked.

"I'm good. Just a little busy, but I wanted to check up with you and see how you were doing."

"I'm fine."

"Yes, you are my dear," Kimoni commented.

"You are so crazy," Ming said. "But I'm good."

"That's great to hear. Did you get the message I left you?" Kimoni asked Ming.

"Why yes, I did. I must say you have been on my mind, as well."

"Really? I hope in a good way," she said with a laugh.

"Yes, it's been good," Ming replied. "I wanted to talk to you about what happened with us the other night. We haven't had a chance to discuss it."

"Okay," Kimoni said. "Go ahead. Let's talk."

"Not over the phone. I would prefer to speak to you face to face."

"Okay, where are you? Are you at home?"

"Yes, I am," Ming said.

"I'm on my way over, if you don't mind."

"No, not at all. Here is my address…" Ming gave Kimoni the address to her place.

"I will be there in 30 minutes," Kimoni said.

~

When Kimoni arrived at Ming's place, she was kind of nervous. She wasn't sure how the talk with Ming was going to play out. It had been a few days since they saw one another and made love.

She couldn't just say sex because it was just so much more. She felt a connection to Ming that she had never felt before with any other woman she had been with. She never believed in love at first sight, but now she was a believer.

She hoped that Ming wouldn't say that they crossed the line with each other, because she wanted to cross a few more lines with her. Ming was incredible. Kimoni wanted to show her how great they could be with each other, if only given a chance.

When Kimoni arrived at Ming's place, she rang the doorbell. The door opened to reveal the most stunning woman in the world. Kimoni walked right up to Ming and took her in her arms and tongue kissed her for a few minutes.

"Well, hello to you, too," Ming replied breathlessly when they broke apart.

"How are you doing baby? I just missed you and wanted to say that to you."

"Well, thank you, I've missed you, too."

"Come in, please. I'm in the kitchen. I was making a grilled chicken salad. Would you like some?"

"Sure, anything that you have cooking, I want to try."

"Okay, sounds good. Here, have a seat while I finish with the chicken. Would you like something to drink?" Ming asked as Kimoni sat down.

"No, thank you. Not right now."

"Okay. I know you are wondering why I wanted to talk to you face to face."

"Yes, I do."

"Well, I wanted you and me to talk face to face about what transpired between us last weekend."

"Yes," Kimoni said. "What about?"

"Well, I wanted you to know two things. One is that I don't mix my business life with my personal life and I don't sleep with women on the first date. I just don't know what came over me, but there is something about you that I just could not resist. I thought about you the first night that you helped me and every day thereafter until I walked into my conference room and there you were, to my delight. I don't want you to have the wrong impression of me."

"Oh, I could never have the wrong impression," Kimoni interrupted Ming. "I want you to know that I don't think any less of you because of what happened between us." "We are both adults. I want you to know that I, too, have thought about you since I fixed your flat. Hell, I even told DC about you that first night not knowing that you were the lawyer she was coming to see."

"Really?" Ming questioned.

"Yes, really. I was digging you. Your perfume was in my nose that entire day."

Ming laughed. "So was your cologne. I held your shirt up to my nose just so I could smell it while you fixed the tire."

"Oh, really? So, Ms. Foster, let me just say, I, too, never mix business with pleasure. I certainly wouldn't want to jeopardize our professional relationship. But, I am not going to let you get away from me."

Kimoni got up and walked over to Ming, who was standing in front of the stove. She took Ming into her arms and they shared a passionate kiss.

Kimoni looked into Ming's eyes and said, "I want you to know something, Ming. I will never hurt you. I just want to love you and share all that I have and am with you. So, if you are willing to take a chance with me, I want to take a chance on you."

Ming didn't know what to say. She wanted to be with Kimoni just as much.

"Okay. I'm willing to take a chance with you. I just want us to always be up front and honest with each other, no matter what the situation."

"Okay, agreed. I'm willing to do whatever I need to do to keep you, baby, because you are my future wife. Yes, wife. And, I swear, I am going to make that happen, no matter what. You are a gem and I would be a fool to let you slip through my fingers."

Ming started to blush. "Okay, baby, sit down," she told Kimoni. "The chicken is almost ready. Let me get the plates so that we can have our salad."

"Okay, is there anything that you need me to do?"
"Yes, just sit down and relax and let me serve you tonight."

Kimoni started to laugh. "Okay. Your wish is my command."

"Don't tell me that because I have a lot of wishes." They both started to chuckle.

"So, I guess its official that we are now dating?"

"Yes, it is official. You are my baby," Kimoni replied.

"So how are we going to do this? I think that maybe we should keep this under wraps for a little bit. What do you think?" Ming asked Kimoni.

"It's up to you, but I'm ready to tell everyone that La'Ming Foster is mine, all mine!"

"You are too much," Ming said. "You always keep me laughing and that is such a good thang."

They continued to eat, while talking about their relationship and what happened 72 hours ago. It seemed so surreal. They had so many things in common, so many similar goals to obtain. It was as if the heavens had crossed their paths on purpose.

CHAPTER TWENTY FIVE

This week passed by so quickly, Rachael thought. She had been really busy with work and there had been a lot of buzz at the hotel. The conference rooms had been booked all week and she couldn't wait for Friday. Keeping the guests happy with their requests kind of wore her out this week.

But, she was glad it was a busy week because it kept her mind at bay from thinking about DC. Even though they had a great conversation, it didn't seem like DC was really interested. This really puzzled Rachael because everyone was always interested in her.

I guess it's time to step my game up, she thought. DC was from a different league than she was used to. She was a famous gay model. All of the other women that Rachael had dated weren't anywhere near famous, just rich.

Well at least she showed interest beforehand. Maybe I should call her because I know she had a line full of women waiting to spend all their time with her.

Rachael picked up the phone and dialed DC's cell phone. After a few rings, it went to voice mail. *Shit*, she thought. She wasn't going to leave a message, but she wanted her to know that she called.

She didn't want her to say that she missed the call all together. So, after the beep, Rachael left a message:

Hi, DC, this is Rachael. I was calling to check in on you. I know you are a busy woman, but when you get this message give me a call. Talk with you soon, bye.

Whew, that was so fucking hard, she thought. *I don't leave messages. I get messages left.* Rachael was not used to making the first move with anyone. The ladies always made the first move with her.

Well, I'm not going to sit and dwell on it, she thought. Rachael began to go over the budget and the ordering form for her supplies. She set up her meetings for next week so that everything would be in perfect order. She did whatever she needed to do to keep her mind off of DC, but it really wasn't helping. She just wanted this day to end so that she could go home and relax.

As the day wore on, she was really starting to get a little restless because she hadn't talked to DC and she wasn't used to women not flocking to her.

What am I doing wrong, she thought to herself. Maybe, she is just playing hard to get because of her status. Whatever the case, Rachael wasn't going to let that keep her down. She was going to get into something to occupy her time and mind.

It was mid evening by the time Rachael got off of work and she still wasn't sure what she was going to do with herself. She didn't want to be alone, but, yet, she didn't want anyone's company but DC's.

On the ride home, she contemplated what she was going to have for dinner. She wasn't up for cooking anything so she decided to just stop and grab something to eat. Just as she was pulling into the restaurant parking lot, her phone rang. She wondered who it could be because she doesn't recognize the number, but answered anyway.

"Hello?"

"Can I speak to Rachael, please?" the voice on the other end asked.

"This is Rachael and whom am I speaking with?"

"This is DC, Ms. Rachael, how are you?"

"I'm great, and you, DC?" she replied.

"I'm well, but even better now that I'm talking to you."

"Oh, really?" Rachael said with a sexy laugh.

"Yes, I was calling to see if you were busy right now and if you have eaten dinner yet."

"Well, no to both questions," she said with a grin. "I was just getting ready to stop and get me something to eat."

"Well, if you don't mind, don't do that and come have dinner with me right now."

"Right now?" Rachael asked in a surprised voice.

"Yes, I take it you are driving?"

"Yes."

"Well, come and meet me at the marina and have dinner with me under the stars on a boat."

Rachael was stunned, but very happy. "Sure. I could meet you, but why don't I go home and change."

"Oh, no, I want to see you just how you are. That isn't a problem, is it?" DC asked.

"No, not at all. I will meet you there shortly. Should I just call this number back when I get there?"

"Yes, this is my new cell number. I will tell you all about it when we have dinner."

"Okay," Rachael laughed. "See you in a bit."

"Okay, you, I look forward to it," DC said and they both hung up.

Rachael couldn't believe it. She was in heaven. "Yes, yes, yes!!!" she said out loud. *I'm still in the game,* she thought. *Let me get to the marina, asap.*

Rachael began to haul ass. She wanted to get downtown as quickly as possible to see DC. When Rachael arrived at the marina, she parked her car and called DC.

"Hello, Rachael. You're here?" DC asked.

"Yes, I am."

"Okay, I will come out to get you and bring you to the boat."

Rachael still couldn't believe it. She was spending Friday having dinner under the stars on a boat with Dominique Carter. *LG baby, LG!!!* Rachael fixed her make-up while she waited for DC to come to the car. She wanted to look good for her. DC tapped on her car window a few minutes later.

"Hello there, Miss Lady. Are you ready?" she asked.

"Yes, I am."

DC took Rachael's hand and helped her out of the car.

"This way, my lady."

Oh, such manners, Rachael thought. *I like that.* As they walked towards the boat, Rachael couldn't believe her good fortune. They walked arm in arm. DC escorted her in a protective manner.

They walked up the ramp to the boat. DC went on first to help Rachael on to the boat. Once aboard, she couldn't believe her eyes. The boat was filled with beautiful exotic flowers of every color you could imagine.

"Oh, wow," Rachael said. "This is beautiful."

"Just as you are," DC said. "Now, come over here, please. Don't be afraid."

Rachael walked to the middle of the boat, in awe of what was going on. She just couldn't believe her eyes. "Is all this for me," she said as she turned to face DC.

"Yes, it is. I just wanted to apologize for not getting back to you sooner," DC said as she handed Rachael a glass of champagne. "And, I wanted to let you know that I am interested in getting to know you if you are interested in getting to know Dominique Carter, the person, and not DC, the model."

"Yes, yes I do."

"Good," DC responded and they raised their glasses to toast.

DC walked along the deck of the boat and Rachael followed her. The night air felt wonderful and, to look up and see the stars under the moonlight was an experience Rachael would never forget.

"Beautiful, isn't it?" DC asked.

"Yes, it is spectacular to see so many stars in the sky. I have never experienced this before. Thank you, DC."

"You are more than welcome. I wanted to show you a nice time since I have been so busy for the last few days and I haven't talked with you."

"Yeah, I know that you are a busy woman and I didn't want to keep calling and get put on your stalker list," she laughed as she took a sip from her glass.

"You would never be put on that list," DC laughed. "But, I'm glad that you were thinking enough of me to call and leave me a message. And, it was a pleasant one, I might add."

"Why do you say pleasant one?"

"Oh, you wouldn't believe the kind of messages women leave me when I haven't spoken to them in a few days. It can get crazy."

"Really?"

"Yes, they, or should I say, some women think that if I don't call every day, or answer, it's another chick. A lot of women are insecure when it comes to being in a relationship or just a friendship with me."

"Right, I understand your point of view, but I also understand why some women would be insecure. Hell, you are DC, the stud model. You can have any woman you want."

"This is true, but when I am with someone, I am with them and them only. Some women don't understand that or believe it. They think just because I'm not with them or around them, that it's some other woman taking their place."

"That's good to hear that you are true to the one you are with, but you have to keep in mind that most studs, or femmes for that matter, don't think like that. It's an all I can get no matter whom I hurt mentality. They think if it's free, I want it."

"But, that is really fucked up thinking, but I know just what you mean."

Just as they were getting ready to finish up their conversation, the hostess came on deck to announce that dinner was ready.

"After you, my lady," DC said as she waited for Rachael to enter into the cabin of the boat.

The dinner looked great. It was being brought out to be served to them. DC pulled out Rachael's chair for her to sit down before taking a seat, herself. The waitress served their food, but before they began to eat, DC blessed the food.

"Heavenly Father above, full of grace and mercy, I want to thank you for allowing us to be fed with the food that is before us. Lord, I thank you for your many blessings that you have bestowed on everyone in this room. In Jesus name, I pray, amen."

"I hope you enjoy the food. Let's eat," DC said to Rachael.

What a wonderful blessing, Rachael thought to herself. *Wow, she is so different.*

They ate their dinner and talked amongst themselves for awhile.

"So, are you ready for dessert?" DC asked.

"Whew, to be honest, no, I couldn't eat another bite, but it depends on what the dessert is."

"Well, we could always eat dessert later if you like."

"How about we go and look at the stars once again?"

"Sure, that sounds good," Rachael said.

They got up and went out to the deck of the boat to look at the beautiful night sky and enjoy each other's company. That night Rachael and DC talked about a lot of things. They got to know each other on a different kind of level. A level that Rachael wasn't used to with her other RL's.

Rachael didn't want the night to end but she knew that it would. DC must have been reading her mind because she turned to her and asked her to stay the night so they could watch the sun rise in the morning.

"It is a wonderful sight to see off of the water. I promise no funny stuff. Unless you want some of the funny stuff," DC laughed.

"Oh, I know you are not that kind of woman. I would be delighted to stay and watch the sun rise with you here. There isn't any other place I would rather be."

DC took Rachael's hand and guided her to the body chair that she had been sitting in previously. DC brought her closer and held her while they watched the stars twinkle in the sky. In just a few hours, they would be watching the same sky, but it would be the rising of a new day with the sun.

CHAPTER TWENTY SIX

It was Saturday afternoon and Nayla did not know what she was going to get herself into. She needed to do some cleaning of her place, maybe laundry, pick up the dry cleaning, and go to the gym. Damn, the list goes on and on.

Whatever I'm going to do, I need to get to it, she thought. *Breakfast, that's what I need to do first. I need to fix me something to eat before I pass out,* she thought.

Nayla was in her kitchen fixing herself something to eat when her doorbell rang. *Now who in the hell could be ringing my bell?*

"Just a minute," she called out as she turned down the eye on the stove.

Ding dong, the doorbell chimed again.

"Just a minute! I will be right there!" Nayla called out louder.

She was more curious as to who would be ringing her bell. Any of her friends or family would have called instead of standing on the porch ringing the bell.

When Nayla opened the door, she was surprised to find PG standing on her doorstep holding a beautifully wrapped box.

What in the world, she thought.

"Sorry for just showing up at your place. I still had the address from when I sent you the last package. I just wanted to apologize to you, in person, for canceling our date. Also, I wanted to ask you to forgive me and let me make it up to you. Here, this is for you," PG said as she handed Nayla the box.

"Thank you, but what's in here?" she asked.

"You will just have to open it and see for yourself," PG smiled. "So, are we going to stand here all day or will you invite me in?"

"Oh, yes, you can come in." Nayla opened her front door wide enough for PG to step inside.
"Nice place you have here."

"Why, thank you. I try. Come back here to the kitchen, I was fixing myself something to eat. Would you like some?"

"Food? No, something else, maybe."

"Is that what you came by looking for? Because, if it is, then…"

"Slow down, baby girl. I am only teasing you. I came for a peace offering."

"A peace offering? What kind of peace offering?" Nayla asked.

"Well, inside the box will tell it all. If you say yes, you will have it to use tonight. If you say no, you will just have it."

"Well, let me look inside the damn box and see what you are talking about." Nayla opened the box and inside was a feathered mask. "What is this?" she turned and asked PG.

"It's for a party tonight."

"A party? What kind of party? What makes you think I will be going to a party with you, tonight?"

"Oh, come on, Nayla. I just want to make it up to you about the last time we were supposed to hang out. Trust me. You will have a great time. A friend of mine is having a mask party and I want to attend with you. So will you go, please?" PG said with her best puppy dog face.

"I don't know, PG. How do I know you won't cancel on me this time?"

"I'm not. I promise you. I won't. You have to trust me. But, I do need for you to do me a favor. I need for you to wear what I sent you the last time."

"Oh really? Why?"

"Because, I want to see how sexy you will look in what I picked out for you, so say yes."

"I haven't even told you that I will go," Nayla said fixing her plate and sitting down at the counter next to PG.

"I just know that you are going to come," PG said as she picked up a piece of Nayla's bacon and fed it to her.

"You are so confident that I'm going to go out with you."

"Yes. If you weren't or at least thinking about it, I wouldn't be sitting here with you right now."

Nayla knew PG had a point, but she didn't tell her so. "Whatever," she said instead, taking a bite out of her toast.

"Okay, I will take that as a yes. So, tell me, did you finish writing the article on me? Did you make me look good?"

"You are a mess. And, yes, it's with my editorial department waiting to go to press. How did the photo shoot go?"

"It went well. The cameraman, Mark, he's hella cool. We vibed the whole time. I can't wait for the issue to come out."

"Me either. I love when an article I write comes out and the person I've written about is happy."

"No matter what you say in the article, I know I'm going to be happy."

"Don't make me blush. You are just trying to butter me up so that I will go out with you tonight."

"No, I know you're going to come out, without a doubt, but truly, I have nothing but respect for you and your work, remember that."

"Let me ask you a question. What's your status?"

"What status?" Nayla answered, puzzled.

"Your HIV status." PG clarified.

"Negative. Why?" Nayla answered.

"So is mine. I just wanted to get that understood. People don't ask. They just assume and I don't want to assume, I want to know."

"When was the last time that you were tested?" Nayla asked.

"Two months ago. I carry a copy of my results with me. Would you like to see them?"

"Sure, I was tested three months ago. Would you like to see mine, as well?" Nayla responded.

"Yeah, if you don't mind me seeing them."

"Sure," Nayla said as she got up to retrieve her paperwork from her bedroom and returned. When she returned, PG was taking a bite out of her toast. "Hey, I thought you didn't want any."

"Oops, you weren't supposed to see that," PG laughed.

"Okay, here are my results."

"Looks good. Thank you so much."

"It's good to know that you are being responsible and getting tested."

"Oh, yeah, most def. I value my life."

Nayla was at a loss for words. She didn't know what to think of PG.

"Well, baby girl, I have to make some moves to get ready for tonight, so I have to go."

Nayla walked PG to the door. When they made it to the door, PG turned around and said, "I will be here at 8pm sharp. Be ready."

"Okay," Nayla said as PG exited the door.

Nayla was just standing there with her door wide open really not knowing what to do or what else to say. My status, she marveled, no one has ever asked me my status nor have I really asked them about theirs. That is really something to think about. But, I guess since I am new, she wouldn't know that I don't get around. *Damn, what am I going to do*, she thought as she closed the door.

Nayla went back to the kitchen to finish eating and to start thinking on what she needed to do for the day. Her chain of thought had been lost since PG stopped by. She had to admit to herself, she was very curious about what PG had planned. She really liked her and was intrigued by her aura. She just couldn't put her finger on it, but, whatever it was about her, she really liked it.

PG was a stud who had her shit together in every way. She was good looking, the whole package. *Damn, I know that sex with her will be off the mother fucking chain. That shit will be intoxicating beyond my control,* she thought. *Fuck it, I'm going and wherever it leads me, I will follow.* Nayla cleaned up the dirty dishes and started her regimen for her Saturday.

~

Damn, time sure flies, Nayla thought when she received a text message from PG. *Shit, I've been cleaning up all day. It's time to get ready for tonight.*

She decided to go all out and put on the extra, extra. She shaved her pussy bald and touched up her legs and underarms. She didn't want any hairs to get in the way of PG getting to her girl.

After her shower, she oiled her body and sprayed on her body spray and glitter. She started to dress. She wanted everything to go in its perfect order.

Just as she was putting on her clothes, Ming called. Nayla didn't have time to answer the phone so she let it go to voicemail. She waited to hear the ding that a voicemail was received, but instead she got a text.

Hey u. 2morrow brunch. where u wanna meet? call me.

Maybe, I'll give Ming a call tomorrow once I'm done with my date tonight. I hope all goes well. But, right now, I don't care about brunch. My mind is on this date.

CHAPTER TWENTY SEVEN

Just as Nayla was putting the finishing touches on her make-up and finished getting her purse ready, her doorbell rang. *Eight o'clock on the dot, she isn't playing any games*, Nayla thought. Her doorbell chimed again.

"Just a minute," Nayla called out as she walked towards the front of her place. She opened the door with a broad smile on her face.

"Thought I wasn't going to open the door, didn't you?" she asked PG.

"No, baby girl, I knew you would. Are you ready to go?"

"Yes, I am. Do not forget the box that I brought you today. That is very important. You will need that in order to get into the party."

"Okay, its right here," Nayla picked up the box and they headed out of the door.

PG escorted Nayla to her car. She opened up the passenger side door for her and helped her get in. She jogged around the car, got in and they drove off.

"Man, baby, you look real good in that outfit I picked out. Do you like it?" PG asked.

"Yes, I do and thank you." Nayla beamed.

"So, tell me, Nayla, you don't seem like the shy type, are you?" quizzed PG.

"No. Why?"

"Well, when I asked you your status that gave me an idea about you, a bit."

"Now did it?"

"Yeah, it did. You have an open mind about things correct?"

"Certainly, why are you asking me such questions?"

"I just need to know you aren't some kind of stuck up, uptight woman, you know. I want you to have a good time tonight. I want you to know that nothing is off limits and just to be free. Do you drink?"

"Yes, I do."

"Okay, cool. Once we get inside, I will get you a drink. This is going to be a party to remember," PG said as she turned onto this large estate that had a gate intercom.

PG rang the intercom and a voice came over and said, "Hello, can I help you?"

"A million to one," PG said and the doors of the gate began to open.

The voice said, "Come on up."

PG drove up the driveway. There were cars everywhere, all kinds, from BMWs, Jags, Chevys. *Wow, this isn't a small get together*, Nayla thought, as they found a park.

"Okay, boo, we are here now. I want you to have a good time. We are here and we will be here for a minute. So, let's mingle, but first we have to put on our masks before we enter."

PG put on her mask as Nayla took hers out of the box and donned hers. PG got out of the car, came around to the passenger side, and helped Nayla out of the car.

Nayla admired the house as they approached. It was spectacular. Little did she know what was going on inside. When they got to the door, PG rang the doorbell and a beautiful woman in lingerie greeted them.

"Welcome to WWPS can I see your invite?"

PG pulled out what looked like an index card.

"Okay, you are a VIP guest. There are no boundaries for you and your guest. Give me your right arm." The woman tied a black bracelet around PG's arm. "And yours, too, baby, she said as she turned to face Nayla." She tied a black bracelet around Nayla's arm. "Have a good night," the woman said as she walked away.

"WWPS, what is this place? What does that mean?" Nayla asked PG as they walked into a room that must have been the kitchen.

On the counter and the table was every kind of beverage that you could think of. Anything you wanted, you could have had it.

PG turned to Nayla and asked, "What kind of liquor do you like? Vodka? Tequila? Which one would you like?"

"I'll have a double shot of tequila, platinum."

PG turned to the bartender and asked for two double shots of tequila platinum. The bartender did as she was asked, poured the drinks and handed them to PG.

"Here's to a wonderful night of fun, adventure and being uninhibited. Cheers."

PG and Nayla raised their glasses in a toast. Nayla took her shots and shook it off.

"Whew," Nayla said as she screwed up her face and sucked on a lemon.

"You okay?"

"Yes, I'm good."

"Glad to hear it," PG smiled as she led Nayla out of the room and into the next. This room was a room that had every kind of drug you could think of from ecstasy to kush, you name it.

"Hey, I just want to let you know that this is optional. You don't have to do anything that you don't want to do. I smoke weed. I hope that's not a problem," PG said.

"No, not at all. I smoke occasionally, not often."

"Cool, so hit this blunt with me and then let's mingle."

PG rolled the blunt then the two walked and grabbed a seat in the front of the house. There were women everywhere, all walking around half-naked in lingerie.

As they sat there smoking on the blunt Nayla asked PG, "What is this place you've taken me to?"

Taking in a hit of the blunt PG said, "I'm going to give you a night to remember and introduce you to something you will never forget." She blew the smoke into the air. "Are you ready for this magical ride?"

PG took Nayla by the hand and they headed up the stairs. Halfway up, PG turned to Nayla and reminded her that once they entered they would remain. Nayla nodded her understanding and they continued up the stairs.

Upstairs was a fuck fest. There was pussy, ass, and strap everywhere. You could go from room to room, depending on your fantasy and you could have it. They first entered a room where they watched a girl give another girl's strap head. Nayla stood in front of PG and watched, intensely.

PG whispered in her ear, "Can you do those kinds of tricks?"

Nayla couldn't even respond. She was in awe watching.

PG then took Nayla by the hand and led her to another room where a foursome was going on. A stud was fucking this girl from the back while that girl ate another girl's pussy, and the girl who was getting her pussy ate had a chick riding her face. Damn, Nayla thought. The expression on her face caused PG to ask if she wanted to join in.

"No, no, I'm fine just watching."

PG took Nayla by the hand again and walked her to the next room. This time, they entered a room that had swings, hand cuffs, etc. All the toys and equipment that you would need for a bondage session.

"Hey, let me tie you up," PG joked.

"Oh, no," Nayla shook her head. "I'm cool."

"Oh, you not into S&M?"

"No, I'm not."

"Okay, let's leave this room," PG said as she escorted her out. PG grabbed a blindfold from the table before she exited the room.

As they left out of the room, PG noticed that Nayla was beginning to feel the alcohol and the blunt. She was starting to unwind, which is something PG wanted her to do. She knew that if she asked her to come here, she would have never agreed. But, she needed to see this and be a part of it so that she could find herself.

If Nayla were a straight woman, as she tries to proclaim to be, she would have never stayed here as long as they had. She would have demanded to leave. That's one of the reasons how I know she was really a lesbian, PG thought.

"You ok?" PG asked Nayla as they found a room that wasn't as full as the others.

There were girls getting down, but this room seemed to have a more sensual feel. As they watched a woman give another woman head, Nayla licked her lips. *Damn*, she thought, *that shit looks good*. PG saw the look in her eyes and started to kiss the back of her neck.

"You like that baby?" she asked. "Looks like it tastes good, doesn't it?"

Yeah, it does, she thought to herself.

314

PG must have read her mind because she said, "Go ahead and get you a taste. That's what it's here for. Don't worry everyone here is clean."

Nayla, not being able to control her urge for eating pussy, sat down on the bed beside the mystery woman who was giving the head. Nayla began to caress the mystery woman's back while she was eating the other woman's pussy.

The mystery woman noticed her and stopped for a moment. She looked up to face Nayla.

"Here, baby, have a taste," the mystery woman leaned over and tongue kissed Nayla.

As they kissed the woman lying down begin to rub her clit with her fingers.

"Give her some attention," the mystery woman said as she gently turned Nayla's head towards the other woman's pussy.

Nayla went in not caring who was around. The first lick tasted so damned good. The woman's pussy smelled so damned good. She licked and sucked as if there was no tomorrow. She went from tongue fucking her to sucking on her clit.

The beautiful woman couldn't fight the sensation. Her body shivered as Nayla's lips wrapped around her clit. Nayla ran her tongue over the head of her clit over and over and over again causing her to moan out in pure delight.

As Nayla's head moved in the woman's wet playground, the mystery woman unzipped the side of Nayla's dress, taking the straps off her arms, causing her laced underwear to be exposed.

Damn she looks good in all that lace, PG thought as she just stood back and watched the show.

The mystery woman began to rub Nayla down the small of her back then down to her ass. She was rubbing it seductively while she kissed the sides and the back of her neck.

Nayla was in ecstasy. She had no cares, as she ate the pussy of the woman lying on the bed. The mystery woman made her way to the top of the bed and sat on the face of the woman lying down. Nayla reached up and began to caress the woman's breasts as she ate her pussy. The mystery woman began to do the same thing as she rode her face. They took turns rubbing the nipples of the woman lying down and making them hard.

Unable to stand it any longer and eager to join in the fun, PG undressed and walked up behind Nayla, whose ass was straight up in the air. PG leaned forward and kissed the back of Nayla's neck, slowly running a line of kisses down her neck.

PG slowly kissed and rubbed on Nayla's back then down to her ass. She slowly slid her hand underneath Nayla's body to grab ahold and massage her pussy. Nayla's pussy was dripping wet. PG rolled her fingers over Nayla's hardened clit then inserted her fingers into her pussy. Nayla's pussy was tight as fuck, which turned PG on to the fullest.

PG laid her strap on the crack of Nayla's ass making her girlhood grow with excitement. She was now ready to insert her dick to give Nayla some message therapy.

PG rubbed her dick on Nayla's clit then slowly inserted it into her juicy pussy. She grabbed Nayla by the waist and pulled her a little closer. Nayla let out a deep moan as she felt PG enter her from the back. She wanted everything that was being given to her.

Nayla's moan let PG know she was in the right spot. PG reached around to keep giving Nayla's clit the attention that it desired, all while watching her eat pussy like a champ. Moans of pure ecstasy had filled the room.

Pumping in and out, PG felt Nayla's pussy juice dripping out on to her. She also heard the soak and wetness of Nayla's pussy as her strap slid in and out. PG could tell that Nayla was about to cum because her pussy walls began to contract around her girlhood's shaft.

PG wasn't ready for Nayla to cum so she took her dick out, turned Nayla around and began to kiss her. PG took Nayla's hand and guided her onto the bed next to the woman whose pussy she was just eating. She then pulled out the blindfold she picked up and placed it over Nayla's eyes. She told Nayla to relax and not to move for she was in good hands. Nayla laid back and relaxed to become the feast for the three women to enjoy.

PG began to kiss Nayla, again, as the two women each took a breast in their hands and began to suck her nipples in and out of their mouths.

Nayla was in a state of disbelief. Never in a million years would she have thought that she would be here enjoying all of these erotic acts.

One of the mystery women moved from Nayla's breast to her face. She wanted to feel Nayla's tongue inside of her pussy. She rode Nayla's tongue like a roller coaster, up and down.

As the woman rode Nayla's face, PG slowly inserted her dick back into Nayla's throbbing pussy. Every stroke PG took got slower and slower causing friction that began to take Nayla over the top. As Nayla began to shudder in ecstasy, PG leaned in and whispered in Nayla's ear, "WWPS. Welcome to the Wonderful World of Pussy and Straps."

CHAPTER TWENTY EIGHT

No one answered their phones or responded to my text messages, yesterday. So that meant, no meeting for brunch today. *Oh well*, Ming thought. *I guess I can get into something else. I guess I will catch a movie. It's been awhile, so what the hell.*

Ming got up and got dressed to go out to the movies. When Ming arrived at the movie theater, she ordered her snacks and made her way to find a seat. The movie lasted about two hours and it was worth every minute. *Hell, it should have been longer*, she thought. *What a great story.*

Just as she was leaving the theater, Ming turned her phone back on. She turned it off while at the movie because one of the things she hated was when her phone or someone else's phone rings during a movie.

It didn't take long before her phone started to ring. As she walked to the car, her phone rang and it was Angie.

"Hey you."

"What's up? I called you yesterday to see if we all were meeting for brunch."

"Yeah, bay, I saw that you called. I don't know what the hell I was doing to miss it."

"Girl, with you, I can image what you were doing," Ming said and they both laughed.

"You know what, screw you Ming," Angie continued to laugh.

"Oh no, my dear, please don't make me," Ming cracked up laughing.

"I don't know why I fool with you."

"Oh, yes you do. Because I pay you well and I love you more, muah," Ming said and blew a kiss into the phone. "Why don't you come over to the house? I think I am going to put something on the grill."

"Okay, cool. See you in a minute."

Ming immediately dialed Nayla's number after hanging up with Angie. The call went straight to voicemail. *Hm… no answer two days in a row? I wonder what's up with that*, Ming thought as she left a message and then hung up. Next, Ming called Rachael.

"Hello," Rachael answered.

"Hey, boo, I called you yesterday about brunch. Did you get my message?"

"Yes, I got it this morning. Sorry, I had to work last night and do an external audit so I slept in."

"That's ok. Whatcha doing now?"

"Nothing much looking for something to eat."

"Well, come over to the house. I'm about to put something on the grill."

"Okay, cool. I'm on my way."

Once in the house Ming started to prepare the food to be grilled. She decided to make some steak shish kabobs, with the steak she had marinating in the fridge, along with baked potatoes and corn on the cob roasted on the grill.

As Ming was setting up the grill, her doorbell rang. It was Rachael.

"Hey, girl, come on in the back. I'm setting up the grill."

"Okay, what's good Ming-a-ling?"

"Nothing, baby, just wanted to hang out with my BFFs."

"Oh, ain't you so sweet? Thanks for grilling, girl. You know how I love your cooking."

"You are so welcome. Hey, can you get the blender down out the cabinet so we can make some frozen daiquiris?"

A few minutes later, Ming's doorbell rang again. This time it was Angie.

"Who is it?" Ming called out.

"It's me, Angie," she replied.

"Come on in. It's open. Close and lock the door behind you, though."

"Hey, hey," Angie said as she walked into the kitchen.

"What's the business?" Rachael asked.

"Nothing much. Came to eat. I'm starving. You ready to feed me Ming?"

"Yo ass is always hungry for something. Come on in here and help out. Get the glasses down so we can get our drink on."

"Oh, yeah, now you are speaking one of my languages," Angie said as she got down three glasses."

"Hey, where is Nayla? Is she on her way?" Angie asked.

"I don't know," Ming replied. "I called her, but her phone went straight to voicemail. I've been calling for a couple of days and she hasn't answered. I'm kinda concerned."

"Concerned?" Rachael said with a puzzled look. "Why? What's going on?"

"Well, the last time I saw Nayla, she was dealing with a lot of shit."

"What kind of shit?" Angie asked.

"She's not in any trouble is she?" Rachael inquired.

"No, nothing like that. She is really starting to have a hard time dealing with her sexuality."

"Umm… I just bet," Angie said.

"She is so stressed out about it worrying about what other people around her is thinking and not being true to herself that she's not thinking rationally."

"What do you mean, she's not thinking rationally?" Rachael asked.

"Girl, she had the nerve to call Kim and ask her for some advice about another woman."

"What? Get the fuck out of here. No she didn't. Yeah, she's not thinking. What are we going to do?" Angie asked.

"I don't know, but I think we all need to just be there for her," Ming said.

They agreed, raised their glasses in the air and made a toast to being there for their friend no matter what. They let their glasses kiss before they took a drink.

They fixed their plates, began to eat and continued to discuss what they could do to help out their friend. They all loved Nayla deeply and wanted her to be happy no matter who or what she liked.

"Whew, damn, boss lady, that was a great dinner. Thanks for cooking for us," Angie said.

"You are so welcome. Anytime."

"Yeah, thanks, Ming. You are the best," Rachael chimed in.

"I try. I certainly do try," Ming said as they finished up with dinner.

I couldn't eat another bite. I am stuffed like a white man in a red suit," Angie laughed.

"Girl, you stupid as hell," Rachael replied.

"Well, it's the truth."

"I am done, too," Ming said. "Now, I need to tackle the damned kitchen."

"I'll help with the dishes," Angie said. "Rachael, clear the table."

"What?" Rachael replied. "I don't do housework. I have people that do it for me."

"Well, the people that do it for you ain't here, Miss Princess. You have to do it yourself. So haul ass, my dear," Ming said. "You ate, you going to help. Unless, you can call your people to do it all, then be my guest."

"You are so stuck up, Rachael," Angie said. "How, the fuck, are we friends? Oh, I know why, I need a bougie bitch in my life." Angie laughed.

"Whatever, Angie," Rachael rolled her eyes.

"Now, you know you are stuck up, girl. Get down here on planet Earth, please, with the rest of us. You act like you don't bleed red blood just like we do. Now help me load the damned dishwasher."

Ming couldn't help but laugh because Angie and Rachael were always going at it. No matter what, though, at the end of the day, they always held each other down and that's true friendship for you.

"Well, it's been fun, but I have to get going. This audit at work isn't going to be over until the end of the week and I need to be on my P's and Q's. I don't need no bullshit to come up," Rachael said as they finished the cleaning.

"I heard that," Ming said. "Well, I'm glad you came by. I missed you this week. Hell, we were so caught up in Nayla we didn't even talk about our own shit."

"Right, I know. I need to get my shit together, too. I want to go on a vacation. Hey, Ming, will you let me go on a vacation?"

"Girl, what are you talking about?"

"I need you to approve me going on vacation, boss lady," Angie laughed.

"Girl, you nuts. You can go wherever you like."

"Hey, Rachael, let me get a ride. I got dropped off," Angie turned to Rachael.

"Something wrong with your car?" Ming asked, worried.

"Oh, no, I left it at home. I was at mom's house when I called you back. She picked me up to help her with some stuff, yesterday, and I just stayed the night."

"Oh, okay. Yeah, you can get a ride girl. Come on, let's go. I need to get some beauty sleep," Rachael said.

"Yeah, come on because you need a lot."

"Keep it up and you will be walking."

"I'm sorry, baby. Come give me a kiss," Angie said as she tried to kiss Rachael.

"Girl, get off of me with that. You are nuts. Okay, Ming, talk to you later, bay. Thanks, again, for the dinner."

"Yeah, thanks for dinner, boss lady. See you in the morning."

Ming walked them out and they all waved goodbye. *My crazy friends*, she thought, *you gotta love 'em.* Ming closed and locked her door. She was tired and wanted to unwind. She still was worried about Nayla. She hadn't called all day.

CHAPTER TWENTY NINE

Nayla couldn't believe it was Monday already. She wasn't ready to go to work. She looked through her scheduler to see what was on her agenda for the day. There wasn't anything too heavy. *I'm not going in today,* she decided. *I'll do some work from home.*

She wasn't in any kind of mood to do any kind of work. She was still coming down from the high that was her Saturday night with PG.

Oh my goodness, she thought. *What a fucking night, no pun intended.* Nayla had slept the entire day on Sunday. She didn't get home until after seven that morning. When she got in, she took two aspirins, drank a bottle and a half of water, and went to bed. *Oh my,* she thought as she tried to sit up in the bed.

Damn, what the fuck? She started having flash backs of Saturday night. *All of that pussy,* she thought. *Never in a million years would she have gone to something like that on my own.*

She didn't know what to think or what to say. *How could she face PG with everything that they had experienced together on Saturday? Fuck what am I going to do?* Another flash back ran across her mind.

Shit, I gotta shake this off, get out of this bed and try to get myself together. Nayla looked around on her nightstand for her cell phone so that she could call her job to tell them she wouldn't be coming in. It wasn't on her nightstand. *Where in the world could it be?*

Nayla got up to go to the bathroom and to her surprise there was a message written on her mirror. It was from PG telling her to give PG a call when she woke up. It wasn't all a dream like Nayla had hoped. "What the fuck? Damn," she mumbled to herself.

Nayla washed her face and brushed her teeth. The more she tried to not think about Saturday night the more she had flash backs. Every time she closed her eyes, she thought about how PG had strapped her while she was eating some woman's pussy. A woman that she knew nothing, about not even her name!

Damn, what the fuck did I do? No need to beat herself up, she thought, *but, oh, I had the time of my life. How could I have the time of my life?* She wondered, horrified. *I'm so fucking confused!*

Nayla went to the kitchen and there she found her cell phone, keys purse and a note.

Here is a token of our night of ecstasy. Something I hope you will always remember.

There sitting under the note was the blind fold that PG had used on her. "FUCK!!!" Nayla screamed out loud. "What the fuck did I do?"

She picked up her phone, it was turned off. Dead, she guessed. Nayla walked back to her bedroom to put her phone on the charger. She needed her phone charged for the business she needed to conduct that day.

As soon as she plugged it in and turned it on, it began to ring with notices that she had voicemails and text messages. *Those are going to have to wait, I have to get my damned head together*, she thought.

The first call she made was to her job. She let them know that she would be working from home today. Thank God cause they would probably see it all over her face, her night of pleasure and fun.

The next thing she did was listen to the voicemails and read the text messages. *I'll deal with that shit later*, she thought, *right now I have to call PG. We need to talk like right now.*

Nayla called PG's cell phone but it went straight to voicemail. Next, she called the store.

"Hi, thanks for calling Frames. How may I help you?"

"Hello, good morning, is Ms. Glover available?"

"No, I'm sorry, she isn't. She is in a meeting. Is there something I can help you with?"

"No, not at all."

"Would you like to leave a message?"

"No, thank you. I will just try back later."

"Okay. Thanks for calling. Have a great afternoon."

"You do the same," Nayla said as she hung up the phone.

Afternoon? I thought it was morning. I just said good morning. Nayla looked at the time on her phone. It was 12:15. *What the fuck am I going to do*, she was beginning to stress.

I know. I will call Ming. Just as she was getting ready to call Ming, there was a knock at her door. *Who the fuck could that be at a time like this?* She didn't feel like interacting with no damn sales person bullshit.

"Who is it?" Nayla called out as she walked to the front to answer the door.

No one said a word. She thought it was probably some little kids playing, but then there was another knock. Nayla opened the door ready to go off.

"It's me baby," PG smiled at her. "Hey, you happy to see me?"

"What are you doing here?" Nayla asked. I just called your store. They told me you were in a meeting."

"I was in a meeting this morning. And all while I was there, I thought about you. So, I came here to see you before I went back."

"I'm just getting up. I slept the entire day yesterday and now today. I still need some more rest."

"I just bet you do," PG said as she took Nayla around the waist and kissed her lips softly. "Are you ready for a round just of you and me?"

"What?" Nayla responded while she removed herself from PG's embrace and walked to the kitchen. "Speaking of we, we need to talk about what happened on Saturday."

"Yeah, it was off the chain and I enjoyed every minute. Didn't you?" PG asked as she sat down at the kitchen counter.

"PG, I don't know what to say. I am so…"

"So what?" PG interrupted looking puzzled.

"At a loss for words. Here I thought you and I were going to a party with your friends.

"We were. They are my friends. What, you have a problem with what went down on Saturday?"

"I mean, yeah, kinda. I had a foursome with you and two other women I know nothing about."

"Okay, that's what a mask party is all about. You go to have a good time with other lesbian women who aren't afraid to be open and free."

"See, that's the thing, PG, I'm not a lesbian," Nayla said.

"What? You could have fooled me the way you eat pussy. Wait, if you're not a lesbian, what were you doing there watching and participating? You could have left any time if you were uncomfortable. You could have said something. I asked you if you were okay and you said yes."

"I was okay. I guess I'm just confused. I don't know. I have all these thoughts swirling around in my head. Hell, I just had group sex with you just 48 hours ago," Nayla said incredulously.

"I know and it was good. So what's wrong? So now you're telling me you're not a lesbian? I can't tell because no straight woman fucks another woman the way you did. What's up with you, Nayla? Seriously, if you think I am going to think less of you because of what happened, don't. We were just having fun. I like to have fun."

"I understand you were having fun, but…"

"But, what? Just tell me?" PG exclaimed.

"PG, I'm not gay. I don't know what else to tell you. You wouldn't understand. You are out and it is what it is. Me, see, I'm not gay. I couldn't be gay. I'm just having a hard time understanding what's going on with me."

"Let me ask you a question," PG said to Nayla. "Was that your first time with a woman? Because if it was…"

"No, no, it wasn't my first time with a woman. I just don't know if I am gay or not."

"So, are you bisexual then? Do you fuck men? Please don't tell me you fuck guys!"

"No, I don't fuck guys. I haven't been with a guy since I was in college."

"Then what's the problem, Nayla? You don't fuck guys. You fuck the shit out of girls, but you say you're not a lesbian? That shit don't make sense!"

"I know. It's hard to explain and I just don't know what to tell you."

"Tell me, did you have a good time on Saturday?"

"Yes, I did."

"Do you regret doing anything that we did on Saturday?"

"No, not really."

"I don't want not really. I need to know. It's either yes or no!"

"No! I don't regret anything that we did on Saturday!"

"Then you are going to have to do a better job of making me understand what is going on with you. I came over here so that we could reminisce about Saturday and have a few laughs. Now you hit me with this shit? On the drive back to your place, Saturday night, all you talked about was my dick and how good it felt inside of your tight pussy."

"I didn't say that to you," Nayla said.

"Oh, yes you did, Miss Nasty Mouth. I don't know what to make of all of this. I'm sorry if I misread you and took you some where you were out of you element. I guess I should be going," PG said as she got up from the counter. "No need to show me out I know where the door is."

"PG, wait. It's not like that."

"Yes, it is, Nayla. I can't kick it with someone who doesn't know if they are gay or not. Hey, if you ever figure it out, give me a call. If I'm available, I'll give you a call back," PG said then turned and walked out of the door.

PG left Nayla standing at her front door, frozen. PG was the second woman to walk out of her life because she was so damned confused. She didn't know what to do. "Damn it!" Nayla yelled as she slammed her front door

Nayla stood in her foyer with tears streaming down her face. *How could this be happening again?* Nayla cried and cried. She got back into her bed. She didn't know what else to do. *Why the fuck did I go out? It wouldn't have mattered*, she thought, *sooner or later she was going to have to face the facts surrounding her sexuality. Damn, I love pussy*, she thought, *and the other night confirmed that for me.*

Just as she was blowing her nose, Nayla's cell phone rang. It was her sister. She wasn't in the mood to deal with her bullshit. She sent the call straight to voicemail, turned her phone off and got under the covers. She didn't want to face the world today and she wasn't sure when she would be able to.

CHAPTER THIRTY

It had now been a few days and Ming still hadn't heard from Nayla. She was starting to worry.

"Hey, babe," Kimoni said as she walked up to the table and greeted Ming.

"Hi, love," she said as she stood up and gave Kimoni a kiss on the lips.

"How are you doing, my lovely lady?"

"I'm fine. What about you? How are things going?"

"Well, just right and even better now that I have you in my life."

"Oh, stop, baby," Ming said as Kimoni took her hand in hers and kissed it. Just when things were about to get juicy, the waitress walked up.

"Good afternoon, ladies. Are we ready to order?"

"Sure, are you ready baby?" Kimoni asked Ming.

They both ordered, but Ming's mind was on her friend and how she couldn't shake the feeling that something was wrong.

"Hey you, what's wrong? You have something weighing heavy on your mind. Can you share it with me?"

"Oh yes, baby, sure, I'm sorry. It's just one of my friends is in trouble and I don't know how to help her."

"Really? What kind of trouble? Is it, trouble with the law?"

"Oh no, not that kind of trouble. She is battling within herself about her sexuality and its tearing her apart."

"That is a hard situation to deal with, accepting who you are when no one else wants too," Kimoni said.

"My point exactly. I just don't know what to do. I haven't heard from her in a few days and the last time we spoke she was a mental wreck."

"I think that maybe you should go see about your friend. Go check on her at her place, baby. As soon as we finish eating, would you like to go there?"

"Yes, I was going to do that because I'm not going to be able to rest tonight until I find out if she is okay."

The food arrived and they began to eat. They started to chat about other things. Kimoni tried to make Ming laugh to get her mind off of her friend. She knew that Ming's heart was weighing heavy for her friend. Kimoni hoped everything worked out fine because she hated seeing her baby so sad.

Once they finished their lunch, Kimoni signaled for the waitress to come so that she could pay the bill. Kimoni and Ming made their way to the front of the restaurant. She stopped and got them a couple of peppermints.

"Here you go, baby, so you can have that fresh breath that I like," Kimoni said as she leaned in and kissed Ming on the lips.

"You are so crazy," Ming said.

As they walked out of the door, she picked up one of the magazines that were on the rack that caught her eye. Kimoni walked arm and arm with Ming to her car and opened the car door for her.

"You go ahead and see about your friend. Call me later." Kimoni knelt down and gave Ming another kiss.

"Okay baby. Thank you for understanding. I will call you either way to let you know what happened."

"Okay, you're welcome," Kimoni said as she closed Ming's car door.

~

Ming drove to Nayla's house as if her life depended on it. She was worried about her friend. She hoped nothing had happened to her or she hadn't done anything to herself. Not to say that she would, but Nayla had been so depressed about her sexuality.

Ming finally made it to Nayla's house. She knocked on the door and rang the doorbell repeatedly, but there was no answer. *Shit*, Ming though, *she has to be here. She just has to be here. Where else could she be?* Ming was getting more upset by the moment. She banged harder on the door and kept ringing the doorbell. She was about to knock again when the door opened.

"Nayla!" Ming exclaimed as she rushed in and hugged her friend. "Oh, my God, baby, I have been so worried about you! Where have you been? Why haven't you answered my phone calls? What the hell is going on? Talk to me!"

Nayla just looked at Ming then turned and walked back to her bedroom. Ming followed Nayla back to her bedroom.

"Oh, my God," Ming said as she looked at the state of Nayla's bedroom. "Have you been here all week? Just here?"

Nayla didn't say a word. She just got back into bed and buried herself in the cover. Her room was a mess. She was a mess. The kitchen, everything was in disarray.

"It's okay, baby, I'll get you together. I'll get you cleaned up," Ming says to Nayla.

Ming went to the kitchen and cleaned up the mess that had been Nayla's tornado for the past week. She cooked Nayla some soup because she wasn't sure how long it had been since Nayla had something to eat.

Next, Ming started to clean Nayla's bathroom. She collected all of the towels and clothing that were lying around everywhere. Once she was done cleaning the bathroom, Ming ran Nayla a hot, bubble bath.

When Ming went back into Nayla's bedroom to check on her, she was sound asleep. Ming began to straighten up Nayla's room. She collected the clothing that was just lying around. She put up as much stuff as she could and started a load of laundry with the dirty clothes.

Ming woke Nayla up, who was still just disconnected from the world.

"Come on, baby, you have to take a bath," Ming told Nayla. Ming lead her to the bathroom and helped her get undressed and into the bathtub. "Okay, baby, sit here and soak for a moment. I will be right back."

Ming left the bathroom to get Nayla fresh night clothes from her dresser drawer. When she got back to the bathroom, Ming sat down on the floor next to the tub. Nayla was awake and she was just crying and crying.

"It's okay, baby. Don't say a word. It's okay." Ming got the hair brush out of the drawer and began to brush her friend's hair. She kept whispering to Nayla that everything would be okay.

Ming washed Nayla's hair and her body so that she could at least feel somewhat better. Ming helped her out of the tub and back into bed. She left to get her a bowl of soup from the kitchen. The soup she was cooking was finally finished. Ming brought the soup into the bedroom so that Nayla didn't have to move.

Nayla was still crying softly. Ming gave Nayla a Tylenol PM so that she could get some rest that night and, hopefully, feel better in the morning.

Nayla ate some of the soup and drank some Sprite before she paused and looked up at Ming.

"Thank you so much."

"Ssh… you don't have to thank me. That's what friends are for," Ming said as she kissed Nayla on her forehead. "You will get through this. We will get through this, together."

CHAPTER THIRTY ONE

Nayla was so grateful to have a best friend like Ming. Words couldn't express how much she appreciated Ming coming over the night before to help her. What she did helped snap her out of the funk she was in and brought her back to reality. She had missed enough days at work and it was time for her to face her fears head on. She didn't know how or when she would be able to, but she knew she had to.

As she got ready for work, she went into the kitchen to make breakfast. She found a magazine on the counter. *Where did this come from*, she thought. *It must have been Ming's.* On the cover was an advertisement for a spoken word show. *Oh, wow, I always wanted to do that*, she thought. As she read it, she saw that they would be hosting an amateur open mic night for people to come and showcase their talent. *Oh, I didn't miss that. I just may go and sign up*, Nayla thought as she tossed the magazine down and headed out of the door for work.

Nayla got to her office and buried herself in her work as she had in the past. She did everything she could to keep her mind off of her problems, but it wasn't working. Everyone was happy to see her back. They asked how she was doing and wondered if everything was all right. She was glad that people were concerned about her, but she didn't want to deal with all of the questions and such. She had bigger fish to fry and she needed to deal with it right away.

Nayla hadn't checked her cell in a minute. She knew she had a ton of voicemail and text messages that she should reply to. No time like the present to go ahead and get that shit out of the way, she thought.

Nayla dialed her voicemail to listen to the messages. Her mom had called a million times and so had her sister. She really wasn't in the mood to talk to either of them. She even had a few messages from PG wondering if she was okay and to give her a call soon.

Wow, she thought. *At least she's checking in on me. Most women would have chalked up the deuces.* Even though she was going through what she was going through, Nayla still thought about PG and that night they shared, a lot.

Her best friends had also called, leaving silly messages and quotes of inspiration to make her laugh and keep up her spirits. *I love them to death*, she thought.

Just then Nayla knew exactly what she had and needed to do. She remembered about the open mic and spoken word article on the magazine cover. She did a Google search to get the venue to get the telephone number. *Yes*, she thought, *that is it. That's what I'm going to do.*

Feeling good about what happened at work, Nayla got home and did some cleaning. She was feeling a little better about what was going on, but not enough to see anyone. She wasn't ready for that, yet. Maybe it will come just in time.

While going through her emails that night, she received the confirmation email that she had been waiting for. She sat and stared at it for once she clicked on it, there would be no turning back. Nayla was scared, but she had to face her fears head on. Finally, she opened the email and filled out the information that was needed. She sent her response back feeling good about it. Phase one was done and complete.

Nayla fixed something to eat, went into the living room, and turned on her iPod. She listened to the smooth sounds of Stevie Wonder. Listening to him always made her feel good, even when she was a young girl. Nayla picked up the phone and called her mom.

"Hello?"

"Hey, mom, it's me. Yes, I'm okay. I was just under a big dead line, that's all. I'm sorry I didn't get back to you. Yes, everything is alright. I'm good now. Everything was completed on time. Hey, mom, I want to invite you out for dinner tomorrow. Can you be here at my place at seven? Okay, good. See you tomorrow night. Love you, too. Bye." *One down one more to go,* she thought to herself.

After she hung up from her mother, Nayla picked up the phone and called her sister. "Hey there, sister, what are you doing? Oh okay, I wanted to invite you to dinner with me and mom. I know I have been really busy at work so I wanted to catch up with you all. Okay, cool. Meet me at my place at seven. We will go together. Okay, bye." Nayla hung up from her sister.

Now that they are out of the way, let me call Ming. Just as she was getting ready to call Ming, Ming called her.

"Hey, girl, what's going on?" she said.

"Nothing much. You must have ESP because I was just getting ready to call you. Like, phone in my hand, fingers on the buttons."

"Wow," Ming said. "We are connected mentally. So, what's up? How you feeling?"

"I'm good. I'm good. Really grateful to you. I couldn't ask for a better BFF."

"I know and you are welcome."

"Hey, I want you guys to come and go out with me to dinner tomorrow at seven. Can you make it?"

"Sure can. Anything for you. I'm just glad that you are getting back to your old self."

"Yeah, me, too. It's coming, slowly but surely."

"I know it may take a minute, but at least it's on the way."

"See that's why I love yo ass, but, hey, I need to call those other two BFFs of ours so that I can invite them, too."

"Okay, sounds good," Ming said. "I love you and I will see you tomorrow."

"Love you back."

Next, Nayla called Angie to see if she could make it. She and Rachael were together and they both agreed to be there.

CHAPTER THIRTY TWO

Seven o'clock came so fast that day. She could not turn back now everyone was beginning to arrive at her house.

"Hey, everybody," Nayla greeted everyone as they entered her place.

"Hey, what's up?" Angie asked. "What's going on?"

"We're going out to celebrate."

"Celebrate? What are we celebrating?" her sister asked.

"New life. New life. Just come on. We are going to have some fun tonight."

Everyone left and got into their respective cars. They made their way to the poetry set. Nayla had a table reserved for her party. They just had to be seated.

"I thought we were going to real restaurant," her mother stated.

"Is there a problem with this place, mom? I wanted something different for a change, a new atmosphere."

"No, not at all, Nayla dear," her mother replied. Nayla could tell that her mother didn't really want to be in this particular venue.

They ordered drinks and appetizers. Everyone was starting to open up. They were even grooving with the poets that were on stage performing. Everything was going great. The night was turning out beautifully.

"Excuse me," Nayla said to the group. "I have to go to the restroom.

"Oh, okay, certainly," were the replies that she heard.

As Nayla got up and walked away, she knew the next step she took was going to change her life forever. As she made her way closer to the stage to let the MC know she was ready, she didn't have any more fear for this was it and she was ready.

The MC got on stage to announce the next poet.

"The next poet that will be coming to the stage this evening is our last amateur poet. She's new to the spoken word family. Please give a warm welcome and finger snaps to Ms. Nayla Ivy."

"Nayla Ivy!" Ming screamed as she looked at Rachael. "Is that what they said?" she asked.

"Yes!" Angie said.

Everyone's eyes were pointed to the stage as Nayla walked on.

"Hi," Nayla said as she touched the microphone. "I just want to say that I'm nervous and this is my first time ever doing something like this, so please bear with me. The poem I'm about to recite, it's personal and it's my life story. It's how I feel and it's who I am, so I hope you all enjoy it…"

Open the door, step out with caution
For this is my first day, out of the closet
Don't know what to do, am I happy to be free?
Or sad because not everyone will accept me?

A new beginning, my future looks bright
That old me is far out of sight
Exploring and finding out new things
I was so far in the closet
You would have never found me

It took some time, about 20 years
I was afraid to do it, was full of fear
Not knowing what was on the other side
Is anyone out there that can be my guide?

Show me what this life is all about
The do's, the don'ts and how to watch out
For not all is happy with me coming out
Must be on my guard and that is a shame

But I've come this far no turning back
No more closet for me I promise you that
Will hold my head up high until I die
Be proud of who I am cause no one can judge me

Not one single man, woman or being
Is going to take this happiness from me
The shame I no longer bare
For being who I am

My new found courage
I didn't know I had in me
Has me smiling, singing a brand new song
I wish it would have never taken so long

To come out the closet
And face who I am
A proud black woman
Who happens to be a LESBIAN.